X

No.

Suttons Bay
Public Library

Suttons Bay, Michigan

DATE DUE

Books shall not be retained more than two weeks, under penalty of a fine.

Every person is liable for the Book he has in his possession.

Take a Body

A Falcon's Head Mystery

Take a Body

John Creasey

WORLD PUBLISHING

TIMES MIRROR

NEW YORK

Published by The World Publishing Company
Published simultaneously in Canada
by Nelson, Foster & Scott Ltd.
First printing—1972
First published in Great Britain in 1951
All rights reserved
ISBN 0-529-04480-3
Library of Congress catalog card number: 75-185120
Printed in the United States of America

WORLD PUBLISHING
TIMES MIRROR

CONTENTS

" Look out! " cried Martin Fane.

A child ran off the pavement into the road, chasing a ball. Richard Fane, at the wheel of an ancient four-seater Morris, jammed his foot on the brake; and the brake didn't grip. The child was intent on the ball, which hit the opposite kerb and bounced back; so the child stooped, to try to stop it on the rebound.

" Stop," groaned Martin.

Richard swung the wheel, went up on the kerb, grazed a lamp-post, and bumped into the road again. The child captured the ball triumphantly, then turned and looked with sober interest at the car, which had stopped, and at the two young men now turning and looking at him. Then he hugged the ball close and ran back into his garden.

Martin, the larger of the brothers, drew a hand across his forehead.

Richard looked pale.

" One thing's certain," Martin said. " I'm not going to trust myself in this wreck again. You can go off on a thousand-mile trip if you like. I'll walk."

" If we have that brake adjusted——"

" If it isn't the brake it's the clutch. If it isn't the clutch it's a tyre. If it isn't a tyre it's the ignition. If it isn't the ignition it's——"

" You seem to forget that it's your car as much as mine." Richard's voice had an edge.

" That's right. You break it up, I put it together again. You run the battery dry, and I swing the starting handle. You may think you're the brains of the outfit and I'm the brawn, but anyone with an ounce of common sense wouldn't dream of taking this decrepit relic of the pioneering days of motoring on a tour of Great Britain. They'd take it straight to the breaker's yard."

Richard listened, obviously struggling against the temptation to interrupt; and when the outburst was over, had the discretion to remain silent.

" And that's where it's going," Martin growled.

He was the larger of the two and, at twenty-six, a year older than Richard. Except for their fresh complexions and brown hair, the brothers did not look remotely alike. The same schools, the same home training, similar habits, and allied professions gave them nothing in common temperamentally or characteristically. Martin ploughed through life with a fixed determination to do whatever needed doing well; Richard sailed through it, doing nothing until he was compelled—and then succeeding with an infuriating speed and facility. If there were trouble, Martin had to fight it, Richard escaped without appearing to wriggle.

Martin sat next to the driving-seat and glowered at the empty road ahead of him. A lock of straight hair fell into his eyes. He had a broad forehead, a broad face, and was thickset and physically powerful. Richard's hair curled and went where he wanted it to; he had a narrower face and was more immediately attractive to look at, in spite of ears which stuck out. He had large, deep blue eyes.

" Look here, Scoop," said Richard, dropping into a family nickname. " I've had an idea. Supposing——"

" I'm not carrying out your ideas. I'm not coming on the trip. We should have cancelled the whole thing weeks ago. Now we'll start our holiday in the morning with no plans, nothing booked up, nowhere to go."

" Let's make it a shorter trip, the old bus will get us through sixty or seventy miles a day, and——"

" I won't go sixty or seventy yards a day in her," Martin said.

He often took a long time to make up his mind; once

it was made up, he was immovable. Richard shot him a sidelong glance, and sighed, as if he recognised that this was one of the immovable moments; nothing would make Martin change his mind.

" What about Pete? " he asked.

" We've no more right to break Peter's neck than our own. I'll ring him up as soon as we get home and tell him. That's if we get home, in this——"

Richard let in the clutch and pulled the self-starter, and the engine started as sweetly as a blackbird in song. He reached thirty miles an hour and then jammed on the brake; the car stopped violently, they were pitched forward, foreheads hitting on the windscreen, and the engine stalled. Martin's eyes glittered with annoyance as he sat back, rubbing his head.

" What the Devil——"

" The brake's perfect," breathed Richard. " Bit too fierce, in fact."

" If you think you're going to make me change my mind, you can think again," growled Martin.

They were in the residential district of Ealing, where they had come for a trial run after a " friend " of Richard's who knew everything about automobiles had overhauled it and put it in perfect condition for the long trip. Richard always had friends who knew everything about something, and usually they were willing to help, *gratis*, in any little problem. The brothers shared a small flat near Covent Garden, and both worked in Fleet Street. It was a Friday evening, and in these side roads there was little traffic. Richard normally ignored speed limits except where the police might be expected, but he kept the speed down this evening; the speedometer didn't work, but even Martin had no excuse for saying that he was speeding. They returned to the heart of London through Hammersmith and Kensington, and left the car on an empty site, owned by a friend of Richard's, who allowed them to use it as a garage for a nominal monthly sum; Martin usually paid. The street itself was narrow, there were a few shops, a café, tall houses which had been turned into offices, most of them belonging to publishers. They stopped.

"Look here, Scoop," Richard said mildly, "we can't cut the trip out, you know. Not really. It's all very well to——"

"I'm not going in this abomination. Sorry." Martin climbed out. "Talk to Pete yourself, he may take the risk."

"We can't go without you."

"I don't see why not," said Martin. "True, you'll have to wind the handle, check the oil and water, get your hands dirty for a change, and if you have the usual punctures you'll have to change the wheel. I'll be at home, having a real rest." He looked at the car with reluctant hostility. It was fifteen years old, but had once been a beauty, and wasn't too bad to look at; he almost had affection for it. "I'm going to get some supper."

"It's early yet, and——"

"It's half-past six, and I didn't have any lunch."

"All right, old chap, I'll tinker about with her for a bit. You carry on."

Richard gave his most charming smile and used his eyes to the greatest effect. Martin turned on his heel and disappeared from the parking spot. He was nearly six feet tall, massive, and easy-moving. Richard, two inches shorter, was lean and willowy.

Richard sat on a wing, lit a cigarette, and contemplated the wall of a building opposite. Then, when Martin was out of sight, he jumped up and hurried away, heading for a telephone kiosk near the flat. A girl, well dressed and attractive, was hurrying towards it from the other direction. Quickening his pace almost imperceptibly, Richard reached it first, bent his charming smile upon her, and slipped inside. He called a "friend", whom he called Tom, talked earnestly for five minutes, rang off, and made another call, which took almost as long. When he came out the girl was still waiting. His smile was delightful.

" I'm so sorry, I didn't know you wanted it too."

" That's all right." The girl's impatient frown faded.
" You weren't to know."

" Sweet of you," said Richard, and walked on.

He did not look round, even at the corner, but knew
that the girl was looking after him. He smiled seraphic-
ally as he hurried along to the flat.

It was approached by a door at the side of a small
grocery shop, now closed for the night. He unlocked the
door and ran, whistling, up uncarpeted stairs. The flat
was on the second floor, and he unlocked this door and
was met by an appetising smell of frying. The room,
with windows at both ends, was long and wide; there
was a small dining-alcove, lined with books, and the rest
was a sitting-room, comfortably furnished but obviously a
masculine abode. The chairs were of hide, the pictures
sporting. The only oddments lying about were Richard's.

The door leading off the dining-alcove into a kitchenette
was open. Richard went through. Martin was at the
stove, his coat off, bacon, eggs, and tomatoes were sizzling,
and he was slicing bread.

" Anything for me? " asked Richard lightly.

" I knew you wouldn't stay out long if I were getting a
meal. I couldn't make up my mind whether you'd
come in time to lay the table or not."

" Great Scott, yes! That's why I hurried." Richard
went into the dining-alcove and was busy with knives
and forks, plates and oddments. He had finished when
Martin had dished up, and went into the kitchen in time
to take one of the plates. " This looks good. If the
cartoon business dries up, you could always be a chef or
something."

" Or a nursemaid," Martin said heavily.

Richard grinned.

" Or guide, counsellor, and friend to feckless junior
reporters. Forget it, Scoop, and let's enjoy supper. It's
quite early, we can make up our minds what to do later."

" I've made up my mind."

13

Richard grinned again, and did justice to the meal, lit a cigarette when they had finished, and jumped up to get the coffee, which was keeping hot over the stove. Martin went to a capacious easy-chair, and allowed himself to be waited on; when Richard brought in the coffee, he was filling his pipe.

" Perhaps you've a friend who owns a boarding-house and can squeeze us in," suggested Martin.

" Oh, easy, but I don't fancy a holiday tied down to one place. As a matter of fact, Scoop, I've really had an idea. I've had a word with Tom Rowbottom. He knows a man who owns a small garage near Paddington. This chap won't let anything reach the customer until it's in tip-top condition, and I had a word with him. Percy Mellor, by name. He has a Buick convertible, four-seater, all the room in the world and pretty powerful, too. Clean as a new pin, sweet as a nut. He guarantees the engine, tyres are practically new—it's exactly what we need. All he wants for it is three hundred and fifty pounds and the old wreck. I confess I agree with you about the wreck, it would be crazy to go out in it. Now this one——"

" Perhaps your new friend Percy could find us a Rolls-Royce or a Cadillac, cheap at a thousand pounds or so," suggested Martin drily. " We'd have as much chance of getting it."

" I could scrape up fifty quid, and——"

" I could *not* scrape up three hundred."

" If you could manage fifty——"

" Nor am I going to buy a car by instalments," said Martin. " We've had that argument too often. You do what you like, but I'm not going gallivanting round in a car which we haven't paid for."

" Oh, I wasn't thinking of the old never-never system. Crazy thing to start. But if we could find a hundred between us——"

" Pete hasn't any money. He's a friend of yours."

" Don't we know it! " Richard settled back more

14

comfortably in his chair. "I know someone who has plenty of cash, and we haven't worried him for a long time. Remember the last time we touched Dad? He saw us through, and suggested nicely that we should try to manage for six months on our income, because we couldn't keep relying on him for——"

"*We* couldn't!"

"I know I was in the red worse than you, but both of us——"

"Out of a misguided spirit of brotherliness, I agreed to ask him for the same amount as you, namely one hundred pounds, because we knew damn well that if you made a touch for yourself and I didn't, he'd come down on you like a ton of bricks. I was in the red, but could have pulled through, while you were nearly two hundred down. Also, of the two hundred he coughed up, you had a hundred and seventy-five. Remember? I'm getting more than a little tired of pulling your chestnuts out of the fire."

"I didn't remember the details," Richard said blandly. "Was it as bad as that? I'm impossible over money, I know, but—listen, the thing is that it's over five months since then. We've a good strong case, too. Mother wouldn't want us to go careering round Scotland and Wales in a car that might fall to pieces, so she'd put in a word for us. It's not as if he's hard up, this business of training the young is all right as far as it goes, but——"

"I sometimes think they made a pretty bad job of you," growled Martin.

"Oh, granted! But some of it scored a hit, as you'll find out one of these days." Richard laughed and stood up. "Let's get back to normal, Scoop. Dad will probably say yes, although he may make us regard it as a loan. The beauty of this is that the Buick's worth at least four hundred. When we've finished the holiday we can sell it at a profit, cover everything, and look round for something smaller and cheaper for running about at week-ends."

" I've heard you talk before," said Martin, looking at his pipe thoughtfully. " It's not a bad idea, though. He might say yes, and I don't want to miss the trip any more than you do."

" I know you don't. If you'll telephone him——"

" Why not you? "

" Damn it, I've fixed the car."

Martin stared into Richard's ingenuous eyes—and then began to chuckle. Richard's expression changed, as it always did when he knew he was to have his own way.

" I'll clear away and wash up, you get on to the Master of Mystery," he said. " I——"

The telephone bell rang.

RICHARD reached the telephone first. Richard always reached the telephone first, by sitting near it or, if he were farther away, calling on some sixth sense to take him near when it rang. He lifted the receiver and said: " Fane Brothers," in an amused voice. Martin watched him, and his eyes smiled although he kept a straight face. There was a quality in Richard which it was hard to analyse: a gay light-heartedness which not only saw him through difficulties but also made others think that he deserved to get through them. He was incorrigible and unpredictable, but not unreliable.

Martin waited to judge, from the tone of his voice, whether a man or woman was at the other end. Richard covered the mouthpiece and said:

" Someone's pressed the button, the pennies have dropped—why, *hallo*, Pete! We were just talking about you. Eh? . . . Oh, pity, we hoped you'd be able to look in for an hour's pow-wow to-night. . . . I say, Pete, the old wreck's had it. Nearly ran a child down to-night, the brake wouldn't work. Martin put his foot down hard, after that, and put the brake on me!" He winked at Martin. " Oh, yes, it's on—we're getting another car. . . . Buick. . . . From Mellor's garage, in Paddington. . . . You don't know it? Nor did I, but Tom Rowbottom recommended it. Details aren't settled yet, but they will be. Where can we get you if we've any news? "

He paused, then cried, " *What ?* "

He listened earnestly, and his brother stood up. Pete Dunn, more Richard's friend than Martin's, talked for some time, while Richard's expression became more and more doleful. Martin reached Richard's side and made signs that he wanted to speak.

"Just a minute," Richard said urgently. "Martin wants . . . Oh, heck, he's rung off."

He held the telephone out to Martin, who took it, hoping that Pete was still there; he received no answer.

"Too bad," said Richard dismally. "He's not sure whether he can make it at all. Some family trouble, I gathered. He has to shoot off home to Guildford to-night, but if he can possibly fix it, he'll be under the clock at Guildford in the morning at ten. If he's not, we're to carry on alone, it'll mean he can't come."

Richard scowled.

Martin said, "It must be serious trouble. Did he say what it was?"

Richard hesitated, and then grinned broadly.

"No. But as he mentioned Guildford, it probably means his kid brother's in trouble again. These brothers! All solid and sensible people ought to dispense with them. Seriously, it's a blow. He would be the life and soul of the party, and with the two of you, I'd be more likely to behave like a sane human being. And he never gets a rest. Either he's working his head off in London or hiding in that cottage of his—near Weymouth, isn't it?— and working even harder than in town. The cottage sounds attractive—never been there, have you?"

"Never. Pete gave me the address once, for for-warding stuff on, but swore me to secrecy. That was ages ago. Tom's the only one who's ever been there, I think."

"I have heard it said Pete has a little love nest, but——"

"Tom says that's all nonsense," said Martin.

"Pity! And a pity about this development, too."

"He'll turn up," said Martin, with forced optimism.

"He will if he can. Well, I've some chores to do!"

Richard started to clear the table, and gave a meaning wink at the telephone.

Martin, glum because of the news, sucked at his pipe

for several minutes before he put in a call to the Dorset village where his father lived. As soon as the call came through, Richard appeared at the door, with a tea-towel in one hand and a plate in the other.

Martin talked. . . .

After a few minutes, Richard waved the tea-towel triumphantly, and came across the room.

". . . We do appreciate it," Martin said. "Yes, of course, we'll look you up on the way. Be there Sunday or Monday. We'll call you the morning we're going to arrive. How's Mother?"

He listened, and chuckled.

"Fine! Good-bye, and thanks."

"You know," said Richard, as the telephone went down, "I'm not sure that I get justice in this family. I'm supposed to be the one with the winning ways and charm, but you're the one with the magic which can overcome the old man's stubbornness. And can he be stubborn! Mother lets off steam, but that's soon over, I can twist her round my little finger. When it comes to Papa—I say, Scoop."

"Yes?"

"Does he ever put the wind up you?"

"No."

"He does me," said Richard ruefully. "I have a most uncomfortable feeling that he looks through me, grey cells and all, and knows exactly what's going on. He's a most difficult man to lie to, he doesn't fly off the handle, just looks hurt. He didn't hesitate much, did he?"

"Said yes at once."

"It would have taken me half an hour's wheedling, and then Mother would have had to go at him afterwards, before he finally said yes. Well, well, the blond beauty's ours!"

Martin looked startled.

"Blond what?"

"Blond beauty. Didn't I tell you, the Buick's a gorgeous cream with a thin red line round here and there. I tell you, she looks a peach, and I'll bet her engine runs as smoothly as——"

Martin put out a hand and rested it heavily on his shoulder, and looked closely into his rounded eyes. Richard stood still, as if puzzled.

" You are a heel," Martin said roundly. " You ought to be pole-axed. Why I ever let you take me in, I don't know. One of these days I'll get over the habit of letting you get away with murder."

" My dear chap——"

" And don't ' my dear chap ' me. I see it all. The footbrake was perfectly all right, you just pretended it wouldn't work. You skidded round that child, took a hell of a chance of a smash, and all the time you were scheming ways and means of getting your hands on that Buick. You've seen the car, haven't you? "

" Er——"

" And you've had a run round in it."

" Well——"

" You knew the only way to get the money was by creating an emergency, so you left it until this afternoon, did something to make me refuse to go in the wreck, and then you just sat back and grinned to yourself while I did the dirty work. You're a louse."

" Really, old chap—I only had a short run. Look here, if you'll just finish those oddments in the kitchen, I'll slip over and see Percy Mellor. We'll bring the bus back here, and then——"

" Your job's the washing-up. And we won't have the Buick brought round here, we'll go and see it. What's more," said Martin grimly, " I want Tom on the spot. He'll be able to tell us whether we're buying a pig in a poke. If there's a poke, my lad, there'll be no pig."

Richard looked supremely confident.

" Tom wouldn't have recommended a man who'd sell us a pup——"

" You're mixing your metaphors." Martin lifted the

receiver, and dialled. " Off with you, and wash up. Then get into sackcloth and ashes."

" Oh, well," said Richard, and went off.

.   .   .   .   .

A lean and wiry young man with a much-burned pipe, dark hair, untidy flannels, and sports jacket, stopped the Buick outside a dilapidated garage near Paddington Station. This was Tom Rowbottom, who, next to Pete Dunn, was the Fane brothers' closest friend. Both Tom and Pete Dunn had met Martin through Richard.

Richard, in the back of the car, leaned forward eagerly. Percy Mellor, a plump, bald-headed, amiable-looking man dressed in a well-cut suit, waited with obvious confidence by the entrance to the garage. Martin sat beside the driver, pipe at his lips, and waited.

" Well, Tom? " Richard was impatient. " She's pretty good, isn't she? "

Tom, who was renowned on most racing-tracks in the country and was motoring correspondent for one of the national dailies, took his pipe from his lips and pronounced:

" Not bad. That is, not good but not bad. She'll stand up to it. She wants decarbonising, of course, and she'll eat up the juice. Personally, I wouldn't take her fifty miles without a new spare wheel, the one she has is as smooth as a baby's bottom. There's a weakness at the foot of the steering-column, wants new bushes and pins, I fancy. She should last another few thousand miles, but if you hear clumping noises when you put on the foot-brake, start being careful on corners. Otherwise, I'd say she's worth every penny of two hundred and fifty pounds."

Richard said faintly, " *Two* hundred and fifty? "

" Possibly two-sixty."

" But——"

Percy Mellor came forward, rolling a cigar from one side of his mouth to the other, and looking as if he had just descended from the pearly gates.

"Had a nice run, gentlemen? I'll bet you touched ninety without any trouble. As for the spare—well, I agree it's not too good, I've a retread that size you could have, thrown in at the same price. Three hundred's fair enough, Mr. Rowbottom, you experts don't know much about market prices, you know! I could get three hundred and twenty any time, but Mr. Fane's in a difficulty, and I don't like taking advantage of a friend of yours."

He ignored the fact that he had first quoted three hundred and fifty.

"Kind of you," said Tom. "You might get three hundred for her. Not my money. Two-fifty's my price."

"But you're not buying the car, Mr. Rowbottom, and you're in the trade, you're thinking of trade prices." Percy Mellor was earnest. "I can't cut my profit right down to the bone for——"

Martin took his pipe from his lips.

"Two-eighty," he said. "Take it or leave it."

Mr. Mellor stopped looking as if he had descended from the pearly gates, became loquacious, became stubborn, became pleading, became sympathetic, for he knew how anxious they were to be off early next morning. Tom Rowbottom smoked in silence, Richard looked embarrassed, Martin grunted from time to time, and suddenly spoke again:

"All right, no deal."

"Scoop——" Richard began, and had the sense to stop there.

"*Mister* Fane," said Mellor appealingly, "as one gentleman to another, look how fair I've been. I came down from three-fifty to three hundred because I thought my Sales Manager had overpriced her, and I wanted to do my friend a favour, for any friend of Mr. Rowbottom's a friend of mine. Be a gentleman. Three hundred——"

"Two-eighty."

Mr. Mellor closed his eyes as if he were hurt.

"Ninety," he muttered.

"It's a deal," said Richard swiftly. "I'll make up the odd ten, Martin."

Martin chuckled again, a deep and satisfying sound, Tom grinned, Mr. Mellor looked more hurt than ever, but, as one gentleman to another, was prepared to take their post-dated cheque. There was one little trouble. To change that tyre he would have to wait until the morning, there wasn't any sense in worrying about it now, when his fitter could do it in a jiffy. Besides, he didn't want anyone to go out in the car which wasn't in roadworthy condition. If they would come for it at half-past nine next morning, he would see that it was in perfect trim.

"Sorry," said Martin. "We have to leave at nine."

"All right, all right, Mr. Fane. Nine o'clock. I'll guarantee it's ready, my word on it."

He offered a plump, moist hand.

A few minutes later they drove off in Tom Rowbottom's new Austin, his while he gave it a road test. Richard was again in the back, silent and thoughtful. They stopped at the Golden Cockerel, near their flat, and strolled into the private bar, where Martin ordered beer all round.

Rowbottom took out his pipe, which had been empty for an hour, and contemplated first the bowl and then Richard.

"You're a mug," he announced.

"I'm beginning to realise it."

"Years too late. Percy is all right, but like the rest of them he always puts the price on. *Never* pay the price asked."

Richard buried his face in his beer mug.

.   .   .   .

"Look at her," enthused Richard, at half-past nine next morning. He had been to fetch the car, and now stood outside the flat and in front of Blond Beauty, which took up a lot of room and forced other traffic to slow down. "The spare tyre's as good as new, and we'll make a clear

23

hundred profit when we get back, mark my words. That the last case?"

He regarded a suit-case, two tennis racquets, a fishing-rod in sections, and two golf bags, which were on the back seat, then the large hand-trunk which Martin had just brought downstairs.

"You know it is, you tyke. Open the boot, and——"

"Oh, let's sling it in the back. If Pete turns up we can fill the boot up then, if he doesn't——" Richard shrugged. "Shall I drive? She's perfect this morning, tuned up a treat, and there are yards of leg room. Most comfortable bus I've ever driven, except the Master of Mystery's, and I always feel I ought to wear kid gloves when I'm driving that. Let me give you a hand with the trunk. Here we go—right!"

His end was easy to negotiate; Martin caught his hand on the door.

"I'll drive while you nurse that for a few minutes," said Richard. He opened the door next to the driver's. "In you get. Guildford in half an hour, with luck; we won't be more than twenty minutes late. I hope Pete makes it. Imagine his face when he sees Blond Beauty."

He set the engine roaring.

3

ALL that Percy Mellor had said about the Buick appeared to be true during the early stage of the journey. The engine ticked over perfectly, acceleration was everything that could be expected, and Richard, always a fast driver on the open road, managed to pass most cars without once scaring his brother. Martin drew at his pipe and was thoughtful; a fact which Richard judged from his wrinkled forehead. They said little until they reached the top of Guildford High Street and purred down the cobbled hill. The great clock outside the town hall, a rendezvous for all who knew the Surrey town slightly, showed that it was twenty-five minutes past ten.

" Not too late," Richard remarked.

" Could be worse," agreed Martin, and looked eagerly towards the pavement.

This was crowded; and Guildford was still the most gracious and yet thriving town in Surrey, with a style all its own.

" More well-dressed women here than in Bond Street," Richard observed, slowing down.

Martin grunted. The only girl he really noticed was standing beneath the clock, and looking towards them. He did not know whether she was really well dressed. She wore a linen suit of dark green, and it looked just right. Her hat, of the same material, was vaguely reminiscent of those worn in the Austrian mountains. She was tall and had dark hair and brown eyes. He noticed her because she was standing where he had hoped Pete Dunn would be; but there was no sign of Pete's burly frame or ginger hair. He saw the woman raise a hand, as if to acknowledge someone, but thought nothing of it.

25

" No sign of him," Richard said. " Pity we hadn't a date with the lady! "

They passed her, and she stared after them.

" Interested in two handsome males, too," said Richard. " I wonder—forget it. What are we going to do? "

" Give Pete an hour," said Martin.

" On the telephone he said——"

" An hour won't make much difference to us, and if he should turn up, we'll be glad we waited."

" Right, sir! " Richard turned into a side street, drove into a road which ran parallel with the High Street, found a parking-place, and backed the Buick in where most people would have had difficulty in parking a car half its size. He lit a cigarette. " Going to have a cup of coffee while we're waiting? "

" We could do that in turns," said Martin. " You go first—no point in us both hanging about."

Richard said ingenuously, " You go first, old chap, I'm not particular. A spot of fresh Surrey air will do me the world of good."

" Plus a close study of the women better dressed than those in Bond Street." Martin grinned. " I'll toss you for it."

" Right. Tails."

Martin tossed and uncovered the penny on the back of his hand; it was heads.

" Some people have all the luck," complained Richard, getting out of the car. " I won't be more than twenty minutes, there's a nice little place just along here."

He turned in the other direction, smiling. Martin drew out the ignition key, locked the car, and walked towards the High Street. He reflected again on Richard's good qualities, and they were many. He lost with a grace which had to be seen to be believed, succeeded in making the victor feel that the best possible thing had happened; and that obtained in large things and in small. Martin strolled up the hill towards the clock.

It was a bright morning, although the sun kept hiding

itself behind lazy, fleecy clouds. It was warm without
being hot. The town had a freshness which had followed
a little overnight rain; expensive cars passed up and down
the High Street; everyone seemed to know exactly where
they were going, and why; no one ambled, except Martin
Fane. He was still thoughtful, and his forehead was
wrinkled; he wasn't exactly worried, but couldn't understand what emergency had delayed Pete Dunn. Pete
had been looking forward to the tour as much as any of
them. They planned a little golf, a little tennis, some
fishing—for Martin and Pete, Richard had no patience for
the sport—and they intended to drift from place to place
for three weeks. Arranging the holiday together in
early June had not been easy—little short of an earth-
quake would have kept Pete away.

Pete wasn't there.

Martin felt that he was being stared at, and deliberately
looked into a tobacconist's window, as if he were interested
in suckers' aids. He saw the reflection of several people
who were waiting under the clock; one of them was the
girl in green. He turned, slowly, and saw that she was
staring at him with intense interest; there wasn't any
doubt about it. He was more used to women staring at
Richard. He didn't smile, although he knew that by
now Richard would have been deep in conversation.
He looked up and down, hoping to see some sign of Pete;
but there was none.

He was looking in the other direction when the girl
approached; he knew she was drawing nearer, but didn't
look round.

" Excuse me."

She had a rather husky voice, with almost a nervous
tone.

He turned and smiled gravely.

" Good morning."

" *Are* you Mr. Fane? "

" Good Lord! " said Martin. " Yes, I'm Martin
Fane."

The girl had a good complexion, wasn't heavily made up, and had fine, chestnut-brown eyes. Now that she knew who he was, she seemed relieved, and relaxed sufficiently to smile.

" I was afraid I'd pick the wrong man," she said. " You were in that Buick just now, weren't you? With your brother? Richard, isn't it? "

" That's right."

Martin left it at that. He was conscious of the fact that he wasn't being very helpful—Richard was much smoother in unexpected encounters like this.

" Pete said you'd be here," she went on.

He wasn't really surprised; and he wasn't wrong in thinking that there was a troubled look in her eyes. He felt that others were staring at them, and as if by mutual consent, they turned and walked down the hill. She was tall, for a woman; he didn't dwarf her.

" Can't he manage it? "

" I don't know," said the girl. " Look here, I must explain. I'm Barbara Marrison. Not Harrison, Marrison. I've known Pete for only a few weeks, I doubt if he's told you anything about me." Pete hadn't, but Martin didn't say so. " I'm very anxious to see him, and he was to have seen me last night. He telephoned and said he couldn't possibly make it, but he might be here this morning, at ten o'clock. I've been waiting since twenty minutes to ten. He told me he might be in a Buick with the Fane brothers—he's mentioned you several times. Do you know where he is? "

" I haven't a notion, at the moment. He said he was going to see his family, they live on the outskirts. Didn't he tell you that? "

" No."

" Oh. Well, he might turn up. My brother and I decided to give him an hour, I'm waiting for him to take a turn of watching. When he's back we could have a cup of coffee—Richard will let us know if Pete turns up."

" That's very nice of you," the girl said formally.

28

They turned and walked back towards the clock, but there was no sign of Pete; there was every sign that the girl was really worried. Martin said nothing about that, took an occasional surreptitious glance at her, and realised that she had an unusually good profile. She wasn't exactly agitated, although her gaze roved about the crowd. He saw her stop, suddenly—she actually paused in her walk. He glanced in the same direction, and saw a ginger-haired man approaching; but a moment later he knew that it wasn't Pete. So did she.

They took half a dozen turns up and down, and at twenty minutes to eleven Richard came strolling along. He grinned when he saw them approaching, and did not look surprised to find them together.

Martin said casually, " This is my brother. Richard, Miss Marrison. Miss Marrison was hoping to find Peter here; he said he'd probably meet her."

" The man must be at death's door," said Richard.

That was the kind of compliment which he managed to pay easily and naturally, and explained his quick success with women; it didn't explain its effect on her. She raised one hand and her face paled. Richard was so astonished that he dropped back a pace. Martin watched her; and wondered. She moistened her lips.

" What—what do you mean? "

Richard did not dot the i's or cross the t's.

" Sorry. My form of joke. He wouldn't miss the trip we're planning unless it were something serious."

" Oh," said Barbara Marrison. " No, I suppose he wouldn't."

She looked round; there were several people standing beneath the clock, but no familiar figure. She was biting her lips, now, as if she knew she had betrayed her feelings too clearly.

" We're going to have a cup of coffee," Martin said. " You stay on duty, will you? "

Richard grinned, as much as to say, " You old dog! "

" Of course. Not that I think he'll turn up now, he

29

wouldn't expect us to wait for more than half an hour.
It's a place called Betty's, all old-world charm inside and
out, and they can certainly make pastries. The coffee's
not bad, either. Straight on, past Blond Beauty."

" Thanks."

Martin and the girl walked towards the next turning,
and the girl twice looked round. Richard was watching.
Her colour had come back; Martin thought it was slightly
heightened. When they were out of the High Street she
quickened her pace.

Betty's was small and crowded, but a waitress in pink-
and-white gingham told them there was room upstairs.
It so happened that the only vacant table was for two, in
an alcove off the main room. There were two tall oak
chairs, a small gate-leg table, an old print behind each
chair, and a window which overlooked a garage.

" Nice little spot," said Martin.

" Yes, very." Barbara Marrison took a cigarette-case
from a green leather bag, and belatedly he offered his;
he seldom smoked cigarettes, but always carried them.
" Thank you."

He struck a match for her, and she leaned forward to
take the light; the cigarette trembled in her lips. She
was in trouble; he wished he could guess why, and wished
that it wasn't something to do with Pete Dunn. The
waitress brought coffee and pastries.

" They look good," she said, but she wasn't really
interested in what anything looked like.

She kept glancing out of the window, as if Pete might
take the wrong turning and come walking along here.
Martin stirred his coffee, and she looked back from the
window, her colour heightened; she had a piquant
beauty. Martin preserved an outward calm which
covered considerable embarrassment, and asked:

" What's the trouble, Miss Marrison? "

It was characteristic of him; no beating about the bush,
no softening up; here was a set of puzzling circumstances, and the proper thing to do was to face up to them.

The girl was worried because Pete hadn't turned up; so was he. He couldn't understand what had happened, and she might be able to tell him something. He smiled as he spoke, and knew that she had no idea of his inward doubts.

She echoed, " Trouble? "

" Yes. If you tell me, I may be able to help."

" I don't think you could," she said, and to his surprise she smiled much more freely. " You're exactly as Pete painted you. It's a private matter between Pete and me, and rather important. He was going to give me some information which he said he hoped he'd get before he left. When he said that he might not be able to get away on the holiday I knew something had gone seriously wrong, he's been almost desperately anxious to start. I think he's been over-working, he's been so worried. Or is that his usual way? I don't really know him well."

" He's not the worrying kind."

" Have you noticed that he's been rather agitated lately? " asked Barbara Marrison.

" You said it with over-work," said Martin. " He hasn't had a real break for the last eighteen months, it's past time he did. There are limits to living for one's work, even if one's a commercial artist. He's as intense as anyone could be, always puts a hundred per cent effort into everything he does, and he's been showing the signs of strain. He has a cottage on the Dorset coast where he goes for week-ends, and won't let anyone know where it is—he says he can really work in peace while he's there. He's a glutton for work, and he's been overdoing it."

" He certainly has! Have you——"

The girl broke off.

Martin finished his coffee, put his pipe in his pocket, and said quietly:

" I wish you'd tell me what's on your mind. There's something serious, isn't there? About Pete. If he's in a jam, I'll do anything I can to help him. So will Richard.

Don't worry because it might interfere with the holiday, we'd let that ride."

She watched him as he spoke; and her eyes were as lovely as her complexion. It dawned on him that she was really beautiful, not just nice to look at. She was in the twenties, about his age, but in some ways she seemed older. She hadn't told him the truth yet, and he was by no means sure that she would.

"You started to say 'have you' and then broke off. Have I what? " persisted Martin.

She said abruptly, " Have you ever wondered if it were something besides over-work which has made him so jumpy? Ever thought he had anxiety which he couldn't talk about? "

" No," said Martin frankly.

She startled him by changing the subject abruptly.

" Mr. Fane, do you know where his relations live in Guildford? Could you telephone or go and see them, and find out if he's been there? You've much more excuse for doing it than I have, and I wouldn't know how to find them, anyhow! "

" All right," said Martin unhesitatingly. " There's a telephone downstairs. Will you stay here? "

No one was at the telephone. Martin put his two pennies into the slot and dialled the number, which he'd found in the directory. Both Pete Dunn's parents and his younger brother, Raymond, lived near the town, and he rang the parents first. As he listened to the ringing sound, he pictured the girl upstairs, and wondered whether she would talk more freely when she knew the result of this inquiry. The more he saw of her, the more he realised how distressed she was; and that meant distressed for or about Pete.

A man answered. " Hallo." It was the voice of an old man.

" Hallo, Mr. Dunn," Martin said. " It's Martin Fane here. How are you? "

" Why, hallo, Martin! " said Pete's father warmly. " I'm very well, thank you, very well indeed, considering my age. Never get old, Martin! " That was the type of joke which Dunn Senior loved; he was the antithesis of his elder son. " Aren't you going off on some tour or other, risking your necks or something? "

" Yes. Is Pete there? "

" Here? Why, no. He came in for an hour on Sunday afternoon, that's the last we saw of him. Surely you're due to start to-day? "

" He couldn't make it on time, and I thought perhaps he'd gone to see you."

" Oh, no, no," said Mr. Dunn. " Martin, I hope you won't let him postpone this holiday. He needs it badly. His mother was only saying on Sunday evening that she's never known him so jumpy. He's always been inclined to drive himself too much, you know, but if he goes on at this pace he'll make himself ill. He's never taken *my* advice, of course, he's so strong-willed. Still, he *is* my son, I don't want him to have a breakdown. Do take him away."

" Oh, I will," said Martin, with spurious confidence. " He'll probably be at the office, or with an editor. I thought I'd try you first. Good-bye."

Martin rang off, and looked thoughtfully at a pencilled drawing of an immodest young lady on the wall of the telephone booth. The note of complaint in Dunn's voice betrayed the relationship between Pete and his family. He was not on really good terms with them— Raymond was the family darling. Pete was too independent for them. Martin took out two more pennies, checked Pete's brother's number, and dialled. The ringing sound went on for a long time. He was about to give it up when he heard the sound break off, and a woman answered breathlessly.

" Hallo? "

There was something in her voice which Martin didn't like; a tension that was almost explosive. It was hard to believe anyone could put so much into one word.

" Hallo! "

It was as if she centred everything she hoped for on this call, and was desperate to hear the speaker's voice.

" Is that Mrs. Raymond Dunn? " asked Martin.

She said, " Oh," in a broken voice; that was all.

" It's Martin Fane here," said Martin. " I wondered if Raymond were in. Or if Pete——"

She said, " Oh," again, and there was a moaning note in the word. A moment later another sound came, as if the telephone had fallen. She hadn't hung up. He heard what might have been a thud, then silence. He banged the receiver up and down with a calculated vigour, and after a few seconds the operator came on the line.

" Hallo? "

" Have I been cut off? I was connected to Guildford 31743."

34

" You are still connected," the operator said.

" Oh. Thanks." Martin rang off, and was out of the booth in a flash. He took out half a crown, to pay for the coffee, and put it on the table as he reached it. The girl was sitting with her back to the window, and something in his expression alarmed her; she didn't move. "Hurry, please," he said. " I'll explain as we go."

He took her arm, and led her downstairs. No one seemed to notice that they were in a hurry. He went along the street to the Buick. He opened the driver's door, leant across and unlocked the far door, and, before she was seated, had the engine going.

She stared at him, and seemed to have held her breath from the moment they had left the café. He started off smoothly.

" Sorry about the rush. I called Pete's brother's house, and his sister-in-law collapsed at the telephone. I don't like it."

He set the car roaring up the hill, swung right and right again, into the High Street; they were just above the clock. Richard was talking to a middle-aged woman, who was among the better dressed. He looked startled when he saw the Buick.

Martin said calmly, " Hurry, Richard. Emergency. In behind."

He stretched his arm back and unlocked the rear door.

" I'm sorry I have to rush," said Richard to the woman, who looked the last person in the world to engage in conversation with a chance-met man in the street. He bent his engaging smile upon her, and climbed in the back of the car. " You haven't left me much room," he said, and pushed the hand-trunk farther over. Martin started off and threw him forward. " Oi! Steady! " Richard sank back on his seat. "What's the trouble? "

" Gillian Dunn collapsed, when I spoke to her on the telephone. Do you know where Nye Street is? "

" Afraid not. It's on the outskirts somewhere, London side I believe. There's a copper."

Martin slowed down alongside a policeman who was watching the traffic with a paternal eye. Nye Street was half a mile out, off the London road, and the policeman gave careful directions and started to repeat them.

" I've got that, thanks," said Martin.

Richard's smile rewarded even the policeman. The girl sat next to Martin, without speaking. Richard lit a cigarette and sat back, watching both of them closely. Martin swung left, where he had been told, took several more corners and came, without a single false turn, to Nye Street.

" Number 17," he said.

" Near side, this is Number 5."

Richard scanned the numbers of the gates of the small houses. Most of them were detached, some only semi-detached. It was a fairly new estate of this extreme tentacle of London's population octopus, but most of the gardens were well matured. The houses themselves, of the three-and-four-bedroom type, were all different, although red-brick walls gave them a look of solidity. Beyond was the rolling, wooded countryside of Surrey; over everything was a quiet which seemed to mock the sense of urgency in Martin's mind. He pulled up outside Number 17.

" Stay here, Miss Marrison, please." He didn't wait for an answer, but got out of the car. " I'll shout if I want you, Skip."

That he was really worried and preoccupied showed in the nickname, used freely years ago, now almost forgotten. Richard got out; so did the girl. They stayed on the pavement as Martin hurried to the front door and rang the bell and knocked at the same time. He stood there, looking massive and possessed of all the patience of Job. Richard grinned at the girl.

" Surprising chap, my brother. You wouldn't think he was all worked up inside, would you? "

" Is he? "

" Take my word for it. That dead pan of his covers the

36

softest heart and the greatest capacity for agitation. Er— care to tell me more about all this? "

He offered cigarettes, and looked into her eyes when she turned away from contemplation of the front door. Consequently, they did not see that Martin had moved from the porch and stepped into the narrow drive, then on to a trim lawn. Here were flower-beds, filled with late wallflowers, which needed pulling; even one or two late tulips. It wasn't exactly neglected, but needed some attention.

" Where——" called Richard.

Martin waved, and disappeared along the side of the house.

" Hadn't we better——" began Barbara Marrison.

" He'll shout, if we can help," said Richard reassuringly. " There are times when it's wiser to let him go on his own sweet way, and this is one of them."

He did not add that Martin wouldn't have asked him to stay out here if he hadn't wanted the girl away from the house until he found out what was happening. Martin was deep; and Martin usually knew exactly what to do in an emergency.

Martin reached the back door. The garden at the back was like that at the front; the small, bright green lawn needed cutting, there were too many weeds in the flower- and vegetable-garden. He didn't take much notice of that, but tried the handle of the back door; it wasn't locked. He pushed it open, and called:

" Mrs. Dunn! "

There was no answer.

He went in quickly, leaving the door open. He had never been in here before—he had met Gillian and Raymond Dunn only twice, and that almost casually. He noticed that there was unwashed crockery on the draining-board, and that the small, bright kitchen was untidy. He went into a narrow, well-furnished hall, which had several doors leading off it and the front door at the end of it. He hurried along, reached the room

37

nearest the front door, and found the door was open.
He stepped inside.

The telephone receiver was off its cradle and lay on the
floor, near a small table. Gillian Dunn lay in a crumpled
heap—she had obviously fainted when she'd dropped the
receiver. She wore a flame-red house-coat, and made a
vivid splash of colour. She looked so still that alarm
flared in him.

He reached her, and lifted her quickly; she was tiny
and very light. Her eyes were closed, but the lids
flickered; she was breathing. Her glossy black hair,
very long, fell back from her forehead, which was pale
and white as marble; he remembered that almost
alabaster-like complexion. She was a beauty, in her own
way; a miniature beauty.

He carried her to a couch, part of the modern three-
piece suite. Everything here was modern and looked
new. He didn't notice the etchings on the wall or the
futuristic design of the pale-coloured carpet with black
markings. He made Pete's sister-in-law comfortable and
put a cushion beneath her head; she was still slack
and unmoving, except for a slight flickering of her
eyelids.

He went into the kitchen for a glass of water. When he
returned her eyes were wide open. She looked at him
dully. He remembered, too, that when he had met her
before, her eyes had seemed clouded; that had surprised
him, for they could have been beautiful, being deep blue,
almost violet. She didn't show any sign of recognition.
Her hands lay limp by her side. The scarlet house-coat
was done up at the neck, and she wore scarlet slippers
but no stockings; her legs and ankles had the same
alabaster look as her face and hands.

He put the glass to her lips, and she sipped a little.
He drew back.

" Thank—thank you."

" That's all right," said Martin, looking quite un-
ruffled and capable of reassuring anyone, no matter what

their distress. "You could do with something stronger—where shall I find the brandy?"

"There's some—over there."

She pointed to a small walnut cupboard, which proved to be a fitted cocktail cabinet. Most of the bottles were empty, and there was only an inch in a Drambuie bottle. He poured out a nip and carried it across, let her drink a little, and took it away.

"Cigarette?"

"Oh, thank you."

She had a rather simpering voice; he recalled thinking how her voice, lacking in character, had spoiled the effect of her beauty. He lit a cigarette for her, put the glass down out of her reach, and went to the door.

"I've left my brother outside," he said. "I'll just tell him that all's well."

She didn't answer, but closed her eyes; he thought that she was beginning to cry. He went out by the front door, and found the others half-way along the drive, Richard with a hand on the girl's arm. Richard was talking so earnestly that he didn't notice the front door open, and his words floated along the drive.

"I still think we'd be wiser to wait for the oracle, Barbara. When you know Martin as well as I do——"

He looked up, saw Martin, and grinned.

The girl exclaimed, "Is everything all right?"

"No sign of Pete, and I haven't had a chance to talk to his sister-in-law yet," said Martin. "I think you'd better leave this to me for five minutes, if a crowd comes in she may get fussed. Do you mind?"

"Can't I help?" asked Barbara Marrison.

"Yes, very soon."

Martin left her to Richard and turned back into the house. Gillian Dunn was sitting as he had left her, the cigarette already half-smoked; she must have drawn at it furiously. She'd put her hand through her hair, which was a little tidier. She looked like a sainted miniature; and she was strikingly attractive. She forced a smile as he came in, and he saw that she had started to cry, but managed to stop herself.

" You—you're Martin Fane."

" Yes. I telephoned you just now, and gathered you'd been taken ill, so I nipped round to see if I could help." He pulled up a chair and sat down; and even sitting, dwarfed her. " How are you feeling now? "

" Much better."

" Fine! Haven't you any help in the house? "

" No, I'm managing on my own," she said. Her eyes asked questions which she didn't frame with her mouth. " Servants are so difficult to get."

" Don't I know it! I wondered if Pete had been here this morning, he——"

" No," she said, " he hasn't been here. He promised he would come last night, but he didn't arrive. And— Ray's missing. He's missing, I'm so frightened."

5

SHE looked as if she would burst into a flood of tears, but spared him that, sniffed as she closed her eyes and leaned back on the cushion. She was trembling. He glanced out of the window and saw that Richard and Barbara Marrison were now on the pavement, and Richard's hand was still on the girl's arm.

She was a recent friend of Pete's. He had told her about the Fane brothers, but had not mentioned her to them; Richard would have said so, if he'd heard anything about this girl. Mystery could hardly be more confusing; yet might be explained by a few sentences from the elfin creature in front of him.

" Supposing you tell me about it all," Martin said, and took out his pipe. " How long has he been gone? "

" A week."

That startled him.

" As long as that? Who else knows? "

" Only—Pete. I told him yesterday. I couldn't stand the strain of waiting any longer. I knew Ray would be away for a day or two, I knew he was in trouble, but I couldn't stay here and do nothing. He——"

" Ray or Pete? "

" Ray, I mean. Ray had told me not to worry however long he was away, and said I must say nothing to anyone. He was—frightened. I've seen it for several weeks. He hasn't been himself, he's been jumpy and bad-tempered, he's gone off for odd nights, come back and hasn't said a word to me about it."

Martin thought glumly, " Another woman."

" And it isn't another woman," said Gillian, as if she had read his thoughts. " Just for a few minutes I once

41

thought it might be, and I told him so." She stopped, and looked at Martin's thoughtful eyes. "You probably won't believe me, but it isn't another woman. He was frightened. Someone was blackmailing him. I don't know why, I don't know what he'd done. He was getting more and more on edge. Sometimes when he'd promised to be back in the evening, he rang up late and said he couldn't possibly make it. He knows how I hate being here alone at night; if he could have avoided it, he would have. Mr. Fane, he was forced to stay away."

"I see," said Martin, as if he meant it. "And the first time you told Pete was last night."

"Yesterday afternoon. I telephoned, and told him everything. He promised to come down and see me. There's something about Pete, you can always rely on him. I felt sure he would come. I could hardly believe it when he didn't turn up. I waited until after one o'clock before going to bed, and then I couldn't sleep. I just couldn't, it was daylight before I dropped off. I woke up with a dreadful headache and was in the garden when you rang, that's why I was so long coming. I thought it might be Ray, and when I heard a strange voice, I—I just flopped out."

"Anyone might have done that," said Martin soothingly. "You haven't said anything to the police, or——"

"Oh, no!" She leaned forward and gripped his hands. Her fingers were cold, their strength surprised him; her face was very close to his. "Please don't do that. The last time I saw Ray I suggested it, he nearly went mad. He said if the police knew anything about it, he would be—be finished. I tried to find out what he meant, but he wouldn't say anything more. He just said that he could see it through himself, I wasn't to worry, as if I could help worrying. He made me promise not to tell anyone else. I feel I've let him down, but this last week's seemed like years."

She looked and sounded as if she meant that.

42

" His parents? " asked Martin.

" I haven't told them. I saw them early in the week, I usually spend a few hours with them on Monday. I don't get on with them very well, they think that Ray married beneath him. That doesn't matter, but I couldn't confide in them. They think he's perfect, and they wouldn't believe me if I told them anything about this."

From what he knew of the elder Dunns, she was right.

"" And now—*Pete's* gone," she said, wearily.

" Yes."

He couldn't help what Gillian wanted or what Ray Dunn had wanted. This was obviously a case for the police. He knew it, yet felt uneasy; he didn't want to get Pete mixed up in trouble with the police, and it was possible that Pete would soon turn up. Taken at its face value, Pete had discovered where Ray might be, and had gone to look for him. He might be looking still. Raymond had gone away for longer than usual, that was all. Part of the girl's state of mind was due to living here on her own. So he tried to reason, while at the back of his mind there was the uneasy conviction that he ought to tell the police immediately.

" Have you any clue? " he asked, pulling at his pipe. " Any idea where Ray went when he left for these odd nights? Or where he was going when he left this time? "

" No, not really."

" What does ' not really ' mean? "

" Well——" she hesitated, and stood up.

She didn't quite come up to his shoulder. She moved slowly, and yet with delightful ease and grace; she was physically perfect, and when she turned so that he couldn't see her face, it was almost possible to forget the haunted look in her eyes. She went across to the writing-table in a corner by the window, and didn't glance out, although Martin knew that Richard and Barbara Marrison almost certainly saw her. Richard was doing well to keep the other girl away. Where did she fit in?

Gillian took something out of the writing-table drawer —crumpled pieces of paper. There were four, in all— cream-coloured envelopes, of good quality, which had once been screwed up and thrown away, then been salvaged and straightened out. She brought them across.

"There's only these," she said.

The address on each of the envelopes was typewritten: Raymond Dunn, Esq., 17 Nye Road, Guildford. Each was postmarked London, W.C.1. He studied the envelopes carefully, while she watched him, as if she thought that he might read an explanation into them.

"When did these come?"

"He's had several others, I don't know what was in them. They never came while he was away, and when he's at home he always gets the morning tea and fetches the post from the hall. Once I was on the landing and saw him standing in the hall, reading a letter—he looked dreadful. Dreadful! But he didn't say anything to me about it. I searched the room after he'd gone to work, and found one of those among the other envelopes. It was the only one with a twopenny-halfpenny stamp, so I knew it was the envelope the letter had come in. After that, I always crept out of bed and watched him; and usually he had a letter in an envelope like this on the day he said he had to go away. At first it was supposed to be on business, but that pretence didn't last long."

"I see," said Martin.

It seemed like blackmail; and that would not be difficult to believe. He knew a little of Raymond Dunn, whom Richard knew better than he. Both were aware that Raymond was the black sheep of the Dunn family, that his parents refused to accept it, and that Pete had a great deal of difficulty in keeping his younger brother out of serious trouble. They knew little of the details.

"When you telephoned Pete, what did he say? Did he seem surprised?" Martin asked.

"Well—not exactly. But then, he's never really sur-

prised by anything Ray does. I can't help loving Ray,"
she went on in a small voice. "I know his bad points,
I know he gambles and gets into debt, there are times
when I'm almost ashamed to go into the shops, because
we owe so much, but—it's not viciousness, he's not bad,
he's just—weak."

Let her think that, if it comforted her; his concern was
with Pete.

"And these are the only things you have that might
help?"

He lifted the envelopes.

"Yes."

"Did you ever talk to Ray about the letters?"

"No," she said. "It wouldn't have been any use.
He was determined to keep this from me. I knew from
the way he behaved when he got them that it was nothing
to do with another woman." She dropped on to the
couch and was beginning to weaken again; tears filled
her eyes. "He's had *affaires* before, not serious, but—
well, he hasn't *lied* about them. I don't think he would
lie about this. Have you—have you any idea what you
might do?"

"Find Pete," said Martin promptly. "That's the first
thing. The second—have you anywhere else to go?"

She didn't answer.

"I wouldn't advise Ray's people, because——"

"I couldn't stay with them!"

"Well, you shouldn't stay here on your own any longer.
Friends?"

She shook her head.

"Surely you must have——"

"There's nowhere I could go without them asking
cruel questions and telling me I was a fool ever to have
married him. All my relatives detest Ray. I haven't
seen them for months, because of that, I've quarrelled
with them all. I haven't a mother or father. But I
just can't stay here alone any more, I can't do it."

"That's a point we're agreed about, then," said Martin.

45

He looked out of the window, and saw the others standing by the Buick and staring towards the house. He stood up and beckoned; they were off in a flash, and disappeared from sight as they approached the front gate.

" What are you doing? " asked Gillian.

" Calling Richard and a friend of ours," said Martin. " You'll like them. It'll do you good to have a talk with Barbara Marrison, and I think you'll get on. My brother and I can put our heads together and decide what to do."

He went out of the room and met the others on the porch, gripped their arms and lowered his voice. His complete calmness was impressive; he seemed to know exactly what he wanted them to do, what would be best to do.

" She's really worried. Have a talk with her, Miss Marrison, make her tell you her story, and then we can compare notes afterwards. Get her up to her bedroom, or somewhere out of the lounge anyhow, I want to use the telephone."

" Orders being orders," Richard said easily.

" That's right."

" Has she said anything to help? "

" Not really. She's scared out of her wits because her husband's disappeared. She rang Pete and told him, yesterday; he was coming to see her, and didn't turn up."

" So that's why he telephoned," Richard said.

" Yes." Martin smiled at Barbara Marrison. " Go in ahead, will you? "

Barbara seemed prepared to act on his advice. Richard looked puzzled when Martin stopped him from accompanying her. They stood in the doorway, watching as the two women met. They could see Gillian's face; she showed no sign of recognition, perhaps a little relief at the sight of another woman. Barbara spoke easily and comfortingly.

Richard whispered, " Your new friend is pretty good, old chap."

46

" Yes. When they come out, watch the room they go into, and listen, will you? "

" *What?* " breathed Richard.

" I'd like to make sure that we don't miss anything, and you've a memory, that's one good thing about you." Martin grinned. " I've a feeling that Gillian's keeping something back, and I'm damned sure that Miss Marrison is."

" Barbara from now on, I've fixed it. You seem pretty certain."

" I am."

Richard shrugged. Barbara Marrison quickly did what Martin wanted, and took the other woman out of the room. Gillian hardly seemed to notice the two men. Barbara led the way to the kitchen, and the door closed; a moment later, water splashed into a kettle.

"Women's unfailing panacea," Richard said lightly. " Tea. Do you really want me to eavesdrop? "

" Yes."

" I shall demand full explanations later," said Richard. " Probably you want to talk to someone on the telephone without letting me know what's in the master mind. You remind me of Dad, sometimes, he has as tortuous a packet of grey cells as anyone I've ever met."

" Scram," said Martin.

" Yessir ! "

Martin went into the lounge, left the door ajar, sat on the arm of the chair, and lifted the telephone. He gave his father's number, and after a short pause, a woman answered in a distant voice.

" Is Mr. Fane in? " Martin began. " I——"

" I'm sorry, sir, Mr. Fane is engaged at the moment; can I take a message? "

Martin chuckled.

" I know the drill. In fact he's slashing away on the typewriter, coining more murders. But I think he'll talk to me."

" He makes a rule——"

47

" I also knew he had a new secretary," said Martin. There were moments when he sounded remarkably like Richard, and this was one of them. " Otherwise she'd know that if either of his sons ring up, even when the muse is working——"

" Is that Mr. *Richard*? " the girl gasped.

" No.   Martin."

" Just a moment, *please*.   I know he's busy, the typewriter's going ever so fast, but I'll try and get in."

Martin grinned, and realised that his father had managed to scare the girl, probably without realising it. His drill for new secretaries had its terrifying moments. He might have spoken to his mother, but she would refer this to his father, anyhow.   There was a long pause. Then :

" Hallo, Scoop.   Don't tell me you're in trouble on the road."

His father's voice came deep and loud across the wires.

" Trouble, but not on the road.   Dad, believe it or not, I've a ready-made plot for you.   You couldn't invent anything better yourself, and here's a chance to be a character in one of your own yarns."

" If you were Richard," said Jonathan Fane with a chuckle in his voice, " I could take that seriously."

" Oh, I'm serious.   I can't explain fully over the telephone, but a friend of mine is missing.   His wife's left high and dry, has no friends, just can't stay where she is any longer.   I thought if you and Mother could let her stay for a few days, she'd probably feel much better. Not for long, but——"

" Martin," his father interrupted, and the chuckle had faded, " Richard's not in a jam, is he? "

" Great Scott, no!   It's—look here, if I were there I could explain in half an hour.   I'll come down later in the day, but just for the moment I want to be able to tell the girl that she can stay with you if necessary.   I tell you, you'll revel in the mystery."

" I make them up, I don't solve them," said Jonathan

48

Fane. "All right, send her here. I'll prepare your mother. And you'd better make the story worth while."

"I will! Thanks a lot."

Martin rang off, smiled thoughtfully, rubbed the back of his head, and wondered if he were being wise. It could be a convenient place, and the calm, probably cold common sense of his father would point the proper course of action. If the police had to be told, Gillian Dunn would be better off at his home than here.

He dialled the number of Pete's London flat; there was no answer. He called Pete's office; a girl told him that Mr. Dunn had left the previous afternoon and wasn't due back for three weeks. No one at his home or office would be surprised if he didn't turn up for a week or two, or if nothing were heard from him. He telephoned two friends in Fleet Street; neither had seen or heard from Pete that morning. There wasn't much doubt that he could be called " missing "; but was it wilful missing? Martin went out of the lounge.

Richard had pulled up a chair outside the kitchen-door, and had done his duty faithfully.

" Quite a story," he whispered. " Nothing sensational, though, but from what I know of Raymond I——"

A scream cut across his words; high-pitched and frightening, startling him so much that he stopped in the middle of a word. Then he acted, and flung open the kitchen-door.

GILLIAN DUNN sat on a small fireside chair in the kitchen, her hands raised, her eyes turned towards a man who stood at the open back door. Barbara hid part of the man from sight, but did not hide his helmet or his face. He was a policeman. He was large, he had a bushy moustache, all he needed to look the part perfectly was a red and bovine face; he hadn't this. His face was thin and rather pale, and he looked startled at this reception.

Richard stopped in the doorway, and Martin cannoned into him.

" It's all right," said Barbara Marrison quietly to the caller. " Mrs. Dunn's not well, you startled her."

" I see, Miss." The constable looked from one to another, then Martin moved and saw that he carried a printed paper in his left hand. " I'm sorry to have to worry you, but I have to serve this on Mrs. Dunn. May I come in? " He didn't wait for a " yes ", but stepped over the threshold and held the paper out to the girl, who had lowered her hands but still stared at him as if at a ghost. " It's a County Court summons, Mrs. Dunn, for the rates. The house is in your name, isn't it? I shouldn't worry about it too much, they always give time to pay, if you are really in difficulties."

Gillian took the paper, dazedly.

" The hearing's Tuesday next, at ten a.m.," said the policeman formally. " Good-day, ma'am."

Four pairs of eyes watched him as he went out without looking back. Gillian held the summons limply in her hand and leaned back in the chair, her face as white as the kitchen tiles. Barbara Marrison said, " Well! " and

turned to look at the smaller woman. Richard rubbed his
neck thoughtfully, and lit the inevitable cigarette.

" What——" he began.

" Why on earth did the ass come round the back? "
interrupted Martin. " It was enough to scare the wits
out of anyone. How long will it take you to be ready to
leave, Mrs. Dunn? "

" Why? " Richard asked quickly.

The missing man's wife looked up at Martin without
any attempt to conceal her surprise. It even succeeded
in driving away the weight of fear which pressed so heavily
upon her. She pushed her hair back from her forehead,
and the gesture was so slow that her hair seemed too heavy
for her tiny hand.

" Where do you want me to go? "

" My home," said Martin, and explained, while
Richard leaned back against the wall and placed the
tips of his fingers together, as if in an attitude of
reverence.

Barbara Marrison said, " It would be a good idea,
Gillian." So they were already on Christian-name terms.
" It's pointless to stay here, and——"

" I must stay," said Gillian. " I've changed my mind,
Mr. Fane."

" Oh, nonsense," Barbara said. " You——"

" What would happen if Ray came back and found no
one here? Who's going to listen for the telephone?
Who's going to take messages? Who's going to look after
this? " She lifted the pale blue form of the summons.
" That's the third we've had in two months, first the
butcher, then the radio people, now the rates. They
always listen to me, if no one went to Court there'd be an
order, we'd be sold up or something. Someone must
look after things here." She spoke desperately.

Barbara looked helplessly at Martin. Richard tossed
his cigarette into the open mouth of the small grey-
enamelled boiler, with unerring aim.

Gillian stood up.

51

" You've all been very good and I appreciate it, but I can't leave here. I'd never rest anywhere else. Ray expects me to be here. I'll be all right. I won't do anything silly again, like fainting. It's no use asking me to leave, my mind's made up."

She looked and spoke as if she meant it.

" Can you get someone to stay here with you? " Richard asked. " It wouldn't be so bad then."

" It's all right. I haven't been well this morning, or I shouldn't have collapsed. I really don't mind it. I wish I hadn't said so much, everything will probably be all right, and Ray will be angry when he knows I've told so many people. Don't worry about me, please."

She looked blankly at the summons again, then folded it up and put it behind a tea-caddy, on the high mantelpiece. She went through that strange, laborious motion of pushing her hair back again; she had a great mass of it, and it was as black as a raven's wing; and as glossy. Her eyes were heavy from lack of sleep and her body drooped, but she was making a brave effort to throw off depression and to reassure her visitors.

Barbara seemed uncertain what to do.

Martin said : " Either you'll leave here, or I'll send for the police and tell them everything I know."

He spoke so calmly that at first the words didn't seem to sink in—none of his listeners reacted at once. Barbara seemed to realise exactly what he had said before the others, and looked astounded, but she didn't speak. Richard put his head on one side, narrowed his eyes, and took out his cigarettes; then he made a faint whistling sound, through pursed lips.

Gillian stared at Martin, her gaze blank until the full implication of what he had said sank in. Fear crept into her eyes, and was followed by terror; no one could mistake that. It was like looking at someone who had suddenly realised that she was face to face with death. She put out a hand to steady herself on the mantelpiece, and leaned forward. Richard moved quickly towards her,

52

thinking she would fall. She didn't remove her gaze from Martin, and the terror remained.

" I mean it," Martin said.

She closed her eyes, and her voice was piteous.

" Don't do that, please don't do that! I'll do whatever you say."

" How long will it take you to get dressed and pack what clothes you need? "

" Not—not long," she said.

She moved away from the mantelpiece. She didn't plead, but looked as if she knew he meant exactly what he said. Wearily she walked towards the door. Martin didn't need to speak, for Barbara followed her. The two women went out, leaving the door wide open; it was rather like watching mourners at a funeral, they moved so slowly. Richard stood by the door, watching them until they were out of sight, then turned and regarded his brother and gave the low-pitched whistle again.

" Martin the Masterful! Why on earth did you hold a gun at her head like that? "

" Three reasons." Martin was brisk. " The way she screamed at the sight of the bobby made it pretty certain she was afraid of the police; now we know she is. If she'd cave in like that, she's desperately frightened, and knows that Ray's been up to no good."

" Granted," Richard said.

" Secondly, she's ill—obviously she can't stay here alone. Dad will get Tucker to have a look at her, and Tucker will give her something to make her sleep—she's just living on her nerves."

" Granted," repeated Richard. " I wait with considerable interest the third reason in the trilogy."

Martin grinned.

" When she's gone, we can have a good look round the house. We couldn't very well do that if she were still here, could we? "

Martin moved past Richard, who gaped at him, and was soon at the telephone in the lounge. He telephoned

53

Tom Rowbottom's number, and the motoring correspondent answered himself. Richard was at the door
and heard one end of the conversation. It was all he
needed to hear; that Rowbottom would come and take
Gillian to Dorset. He stood with his hands in his pocket
until the call was finished, and when Martin turned
round, he said faintly:

"I need a drink. This is a new Martin. I've always
known you had a capacity for the unexpected, but
this——"

"Don't be an ass. It's quite simple. There's something badly wrong, Pete's mixed up in it, and if it's
possible to save him a lot of trouble, I'll do it. There's
plenty of room for Gillian at home, and she'll be safe
there for a bit. Tom will be able to run her down to
Dorset and get back to town tonight. All we have to
arrange now is for someone to sleep at this place. Would
you——"

"I would not." Richard was emphatic. "I am on
the first leg of a motoring holiday. Remember?"

"Our plans have changed," said Martin calmly.
"Until we find Pete, we can't really start. Taken by and
large, I suppose the sensible thing would be to tell the
police, but I'm not keen. Are you?"

"You're the law-abiding member of this brotherhood."

"Supposing you stop being flippant," said Martin,
with an edge to his voice.

"Sorry. I'm suffering from shock, old chap."
Richard straightened up. "I'll give it a run before we
send for the police, if only for Pete's sake. He probably
knows his nice kid brother has got himself into a nasty
jam, and would like to get him out. You know, you can
now be thankful that some people are cursed worse than
you are, even with brothers!" His grin was impish,
and a delight. "So you think we ought to start by
searching this place?"

"I think Gillian could have told us more."

"You think the same about Barbara, apparently."

"Oh, yes." Martin was casual. "I wouldn't take Barbara too much for granted yet." He took out his pipe and began to rub the bowl with his great palm. "What did they say to each other?"

There was no substantial difference between what Gillian had told Barbara and what she had told Martin; certainly nothing to suggest that she had kept anything back. Barbara Marrison had made no useful contribution to the conversation; she had, said Richard, made sympathetic noises, which had stopped with the arrival of the policeman.

"We'll have a chat with Barbara when Gillian's gone," said Martin. "Meanwhile——"

"You know, you'll put yourself in her bad books if you become too masterful."

"So long as you don't, why worry? What we have to find out is why Pete was prepared to meet Barbara under the clock and see her for a few minutes, whether she has anything to do with the Raymond mystery, and whether Barbara can give us any idea where to find Pete. Also, we have to find someone who'll look after this place while Gillian's away."

The last was in a troubled voice.

"Getting worried?" Richard asked. "Just wave a wand like you did with Tom, and you'll get someone to volunteer for that, as he volunteered to take Gillian home. I think you're biting off too much, Scoop. Seriously."

"Probably you're right. But——"

The telephone bell rang. At the first slight ting, Martin snatched the receiver; the bell had hardly sounded. The speed of his movement surprised his brother, but Richard didn't take long to see the reason why, and tip-toed towards the stairs; there was no sound from the upper floor, nothing to suggest that Gillian had heard the bell. He closed the door, and stood with his back against it, as Martin spoke into the mouthpiece in a husky whisper.

"Hallo?"

" Hold on, please, I've a call for you."

Martin waited, and heard the operator say, " Press button A, please, caller, you're through." He heard the sound of the money dropping into the call-box; so this was a toll or trunk call, not local. Next he heard a man's voice, hoarse and urgent:

" That you, Gill? "

" Pete! " exclaimed Martin, in a hushed voice. " What the devil are you up to? Where are you? Why——"

" *Martin !* "

" Yes. What——"

" Why are you there? " Pete Dunn countered; he sounded almost breathless. " Is Gill all right? Is she——"

" Yes. She's as worried as blazes."

" Get her away from there," said Pete urgently. " Never mind where you take her, get her away. She's not safe at that place. I——"

" Where are you? What's it about? The police ought to know if——"

" No! " Pete's voice was sharp. " No, don't do that yet, I won't leave it too late. Ray's got himself into a shocking mess, I'd like to keep him away from the police if I can. Just take Gill away. 'Bye."

He rang off before Martin could say another word.

As Martin replaced the telephone, Richard straightened up from the door, walked across and rested a hand on Martin's shoulder. He shook his head, slowly. Martin looked at him as if he hardly realised that anyone was there. No sound came from above their heads or from outside. The sun shone brightly, and it was getting warmer.

" I have always believed you were cut out to be a hero," Richard declared. "I'm not so sure you're a master detective. I know how your solemn mind ticks over and how you love thinking deep thoughts without sharing them, but we're in this together. As a pair, we might do a nice job of detection. Besides, if we get into trouble with the police, we can blame each other and confuse them in the Master of Mystery's best style. If you shoot a line on your own, you'll be in a cleft stick, as it were. What did Pete say? "

" Raymond's in a shocking mess."

" As if we didn't know. What else? "

" He really rang up to tell Gillian to get away from here," said Martin, and his lips began to curve. " He seemed quite anxious about it."

Richard backed a pace, and looked apprehensive.

" Great Scott! Have you become psychic? "

" Not yet."

" Or——" Richard paused, and stopped putting up an act, looked genuinely taken aback, as if some new thought had shaken him badly. He stubbed out his cigarette and looked at Martin with a different expression; his voice also changed its tone; when in the mood he could be as serious as anyone. " Or did you know something about this before, without telling me? Out with it, Scoop."

Martin grinned broadly.

" No, it's as new to me as to you. I just had a feeling that it would be a good thing to get Gillian out of here. So has Pete. If Pete's worried because she's staying here, it means one of two things. Care to guess? "

" I'll just listen and marvel."

" That will be a nice change for you. Either he thinks she might be in danger, or he wants her out of the way, so that he or someone else can come here when she isn't about."

" Ah," said Richard. " Possibly. Probably. I withdraw my remarks about your aptitude for detection, you obviously have a mind for it. If you go on much longer, I shall begin to believe that you've committed the heinous crime of reading some of Dad's books. Who's going to stay here, to find out what happens? "

" I am."

" You have a kid brother. Remember? "

" I sometimes wish I could forget. You'll look after Barbara Marrison and like it. We don't want her here."

" Now you're playing on my home ground," said Richard brightly. " My psychology as applied to the female sex tells me that Barbara won't be put off so easily. I had a merry job keeping her outside while you did your piece with Gillian. She is worried about Pete. I don't know how well she knows him, but she's desperately anxious to see him. And——"

" That's where you come in. You'll take her to all his usual haunts and spend the rest of the morning and the early afternoon looking for him. I'll simply stay here kicking my heels until you come back."

" Oh," said Richard. " Serious? "

" I am."

" I suppose it's the right thing to do, too." Richard brightened. " Well, I can imagine worse ways of spend-

58

ing a few hours, if I can once get her mind off Pete she should be scintillating company. Those eyes! I'll have to try to thaw her out. And what time would you like me back, sir?"

"Aim for four o'clock," said Martin. "If anything's going to happen here, it will probably happen to-day. Pete wouldn't have tried to scare Gillian off about something that might happen to-morrow. Given much thought to Pete, lately?" he added thoughtfully.

"He's been a bear with a sore head a lot of the time. Overwork. Do you think it was something beside overwork?"

"I didn't, but I do now." Martin moved away from the telephone. "I hope we're doing the right thing in keeping all this from the police."

"Of course we're not!"

Martin looked rueful.

"On the other hand," said Richard reasoningly, "what have we to take to the police? Raymond's disappeared for a week. He isn't the first man to have left his wife as miserable as a babe without its rattle, is he? He's in money trouble, too, so has plenty of excuse for wanting to slide out. There's been no crime committed, as far as we know. Pete let us down by failing to arrive, and now says that Raymond's in a jam. We don't know what kind of jam. True, Gillian's afraid to go to the police, and screamed at the sight of a man in blue, but anyone in a nervous condition might do that. And it would be normal enough for her to say 'no police' if she thought Raymond had gone off with a popsie. If you're worrying about whether the police would come down with a heavy hand because we're being discreet, you needn't. We've spotted no crime or criminal. If you're just being worried by your conscience——" Richard chuckled. "There's nothing I can do about that, I wouldn't dream of coming between you and your conscience! It's much too massive for me."

Martin kept smoothing the bowl of his pipe.

59

Richard drew a deep breath, and when he spoke again, his voice sounded like Martin's, deeper than his own, and giving forth with great deliberation, as if he were thinking as he talked.

" The issue, old chap, is to decide what is the right thing to do. Having decided—go and do it. How can we best help Pete and Gillian? By going to the police? Or by staying away? That's the question."

Martin gave a slow, amused grin.

" I'll tan the hide off you, one of these days. We'll decide what to do to-night."

.   .   .   .

Martin went to the gate as Rowbottom arrived, and told him everything that had happened, while Tom puffed at his pipe.

" I did wonder if Pete's gone to this cottage of his," Martin said. " I don't suppose it's on the phone, but——"

" When I've delivered the goods to your home, I'll go and have a look," said Tom. " And I'll find someone down there to watch the cottage and telephone if Pete turns up."

" Good! "

Martin went back to the house, and soon Gillian Dunn, with Barbara by her side, walked along the garden-path, looking like a wraith. Wearing a light-weight, cream-coloured coat, hatless, and carrying a large red hand-bag, she moved slowly and steadily towards the gate and Tom Rowbottom, who stood by the side of the gleaming black Austin.

With her hair piled up high, so that she looked top heavy, Gillian reached the gate and climbed into the car, next to Rowbottom. Richard put her case in the back, Barbara closed her door, and Tom took the wheel. Martin stood in the porch of the house, watching.

The car moved off. Barbara and Richard waited until it had turned the corner. The girl didn't once turn round to look at the house. The noise of the engine

60

faded, and Richard offered Barbara a cigarette as they drew near the porch.

" Not now, thanks."

Richard lit up.

" Hallo, Scoop! Now you've got your own way and Gillian's off the premises, what now? "

Martin appeared to consider the question. Barbara watched him intently.

" Seems to me that one of us must stay here, and that one of us ought to look for Pete," he said. " We could try his office, his club, several other places in town. You know his friends as well as I do, you could look them up. Care to go with Richard, Barbara? "

It was the first time he had used her Christian name; he seemed to savour it.

" Will it help? " She seemed eager. " I must see him, if it's possible."

" We can't tell whether it will help. It'll have to be done." Martin had said nothing to her about Pete's telephone call, and knew that he could rely on Richard not to mention it. " It's possible that Raymond will turn up, and certainly one of us ought to stay here. You like dashing about more than I, Richard. Agreed? "

" Suits me. Coming, Barbara? "

" Yes. Yes, I think I will. When shall we start? "

" Now," said Martin, and his eyes gleamed. " Make sure that he's careful driving that blond brute outside. He's always a danger on the road, and if he tries to keep one eye on you and the other on the traffic, you'll end up in hospital. Otherwise I think you'll be quite safe with him."

Barbara laughed. That was a good thing to hear, and made her good to see. Until then she had been burdened by a weight of anxiety, and that had shown in her face. For a moment the burden lifted, her eyes cleared, she laughed because she was amused. It gave added vitality to her beauty, and Martin watched her closely, drawing at his pipe.

61

" I shall deal with you when we're alone," Richard said weakly. " Coming, Barbara? "

He took her arm.

Martin watched them walking towards the Buick, Richard talking earnestly. They waved as the car moved off. Martin didn't wait until it was out of sight, but turned into the house and closed the front door. He went into the lounge and dropped into an easy-chair. Now that he was alone, the sense of excitement disappeared. He couldn't quite understand that; he had schemed to be here alone because he thought it would be a good thing to look round, and to receive anyone who might come to play some funny tricks with Gillian. Now, he felt flat. When he shifted his position, he remembered Richard and Barbara standing in front of him, in the porch; and Richard's face gradually faded, leaving only Barbara. He remembered her exactly as she had been when she had laughed. He had enjoyed looking at her; he did not remember having felt quite the same when looking at a girl. He stood up, abruptly.

" Shake out of it," he said—and then glanced at a small table, near the door; and saw a hand-bag. It was Barbara's green leather one.

He stood still.

It wasn't surprising that she had forgotten it; she hadn't been thinking much about what she had been doing. She probably wouldn't miss it until she needed something out of it, and that would probably be when they were running into London. With their programme in mind, neither of them would feel like turning back, unless there was something in the bag which Barbara would think important. As the thoughts flashed through his mind, he went across to the hand-bag and picked it up. Like her clothes, and like the girl herself, it had quality. There was a large brass clasp. He had only to open the clasp to look inside. He didn't open it.

Richard, with his knack of hitting the spot, had teased him with the amiable gibe that he imagined himself a hero in one of his father's mystery stories. That was at least half true. He took those stories more seriously than Richard. They were extremely popular, and Jonathan Fane had a huge public, but they weren't true to life. The characters were larger than life and the incidents often improbable. The stories wouldn't bear close examination, but at times Martin had wondered how he would behave if faced by a set of circumstances like those imagined by his father. The circumstances were here; he had the chance to test his own reaction. His father would probably tell him he had acted true to the cardboard-hero type, by deciding not to go to the police. Probably he'd been true to that type—which didn't exist in the way he had handled Gillian Dunn. Now he had another test. He smiled wryly as he looked at the hand-bag.

Put one of the story-book heroes into his place; what would the character do? Already he, Martin Fane, had let himself think that Barbara Marrison knew more than she had pretended; he was quite sure of it. When she had reacted so oddly to Richard's careless: "The man must be at death's door" she had virtually told Martin that she had reason to be afraid that Pete was in danger.

Or was that simply imagination?

A creation of his father wouldn't be in a moment's doubt. Whatever he thought of Barbara Marrison as a person, he would put her on the list of suspects and would open that hand-bag. He'd have no scruples and no conscience about it. If all ran true to his father's form, there would be something of vital interest in there; probably something incriminating, or at least evidence that pointed suspicion at her.

Suspicion of what?

He picked up the bag and dropped it into a chair, breathed: "Oh, rot!" and looked round the room. Then he started to search the writing-table; there was only one drawer, and it wasn't locked. Most of the papers in it were bills and dunning letters; Raymond must owe several hundreds of pounds. From what Martin knew of him, he had a good job and an independent income. The house was smaller than he might have been expected to own. Certainly there was no reason why he should be so heavily in debt, except that he was known to be a great gambler. If one added blackmail, and the evidence pointed to it, there wasn't much need to look farther for an explanation.

Nothing in the drawer offered any help.

He went into the dining-room.

After the first flush of excitement he found this search distasteful. Poking about in other people's private possessions wasn't palatable. Was it in fact serving any good purpose? He found nothing in the dining-room, although he started to take the books out of a corner bookcase. He pushed them all back with a sudden flare of annoyance. To search every nook would take hours; it wasn't practicable, and would almost certainly prove to be a waste of time. He could now tell his father a thing or two about what it felt like to be an amateur detective!

He went upstairs.

He would never know what prompted him to go straight to the walnut wardrobe and open the door and look in the corner, beneath Gillian's clothes. As she was short, there was plenty of room at the foot, much more than usual. He saw a small attaché case and an ordinary black metal deed-box. The deed-box, with the lock showing, was underneath the attaché case. A shaft of sunlight shone through the window and showed on the brass fitting; it would have been impossible not to see that someone had tried to force it. The black enamel round the lock was badly scratched, and there were several dents.

He bent down to pick it up.

He stopped abruptly and looked at his fingers, grinned in a way which would have reminded anyone who knew them of Richard, took out a handkerchief

64

and spread it over his hand. He found it surprisingly difficult to get a hold on the box that way, but it would not leave finger-prints. He took the box to the dressing-table and let it fall; it knocked over a glass candlestick. The dressing-table was messy, with a dusting of powder, combs containing some of Gillian's black hairs, odd pieces of cotton-wool stained red with lipstick, and a heap of cigarette-ends on two ash-trays and a saucer. Gillian had gone all to pieces, or she wouldn't have left the place in this state.

He studied the box.

It certainly hadn't been opened; as certainly, someone had tried to force it. The quick grin curved his lips again. He looked at the handle of a hair-brush, breathed on it, and saw the way finger-prints showed up; all were quite small—Gillian's, no doubt. Then he breathed on the surface of the deed-box. There were some larger prints, which only just showed up; but the smaller ones were on the box, too, and they appeared to have been superimposed on the others.

Had Gillian tried to open this, but found it beyond her strength?

He stood up, looking at himself in the mirror, but imagined his father's face, not his. What would the Maestro have his hero do now? Force the box, of course; but without leaving finger-prints. He had no gloves; he never wore them. He turned round abruptly, went into the bathroom, and in a cabinet found a spool of adhesive tape. He cut off a few strips and stuck them over his finger-tips; it took a surprising time, but he could now handle anything he wanted to without leaving a print.

He conjured up a picture of his father, chuckled aloud, wiped the scissors with a sponge, and turned towards the bedroom. As he neared the door, he saw a man creeping up the stairs.

MARTIN backed a pace and held his breath.

He had heard no sound, and heard none now. He could no longer see the man, only the landing and the open bedroom door. He took a long step towards the wall behind the door, and wondered if his shoes would squeak on the rubber flooring; they didn't. His heart thumped like a trip-hammer. He pressed against the wall, wondering almost desperately if the man would look into the bathroom. He himself had no weapon. Then he saw the bathroom stool within reach. He stretched out and picked it up, nearly dropped it, and grabbed with his other hand. He saved it from falling, but didn't know whether he had averted making a noise.

It would not have been so bad but for the gun which he'd seen in the stranger's right hand.

He could picture the man vividly.

He was small and dark-haired, with a rather round face and a snub nose. Well-dressed, as far as Martin could judge, he was rather a nondescript individual; his lips had been parted, and he had held the small gun snugly. Because he had been staring at the open bedroom door, he had failed to see Martin.

Martin heard a faint sound; a footstep. Then the man passed the door, still looking towards the bedroom. He stopped abruptly and caught his breath, as if he had seen something to alarm him.

Martin tightened his grip on the stool.

The man didn't turn round, but went towards the bedroom and stepped inside. He went cautiously, leaning to one side obviously in order to see the dressing-table and all corners of the room. He seemed to be satisfied that no one was about, and went forward more firmly; his footsteps were quite audible.

He *laughed.*

Martin stepped forward, to see him more clearly, and still held the stool. His thumping heart suddenly steadied, for the man put his gun into his pocket. Martin grinned. The man went farther forward, and bent over the dressing-table—and laughed again; it was impossible to miss the note of triumph in that laugh.

He picked up the deed-box, and tried the lock. Then he turned round.

Martin was already in the doorway, with the stool poised as a weapon. The man dropped the box, which crashed on to the floor, and flashed his right hand towards his pocket. Martin flung the stool at his stomach and jumped forward desperately; but he had no need to worry. The stool caught the man in the side and sent him staggering before he could get at his gun. He knocked against the side of the bed, and fell awkwardly. Martin gripped his right wrist, held the arm up, and dipped into his pocket.

The gun was a lethal weapon, all right: a .32 Smithson. Martin dropped it into his own pocket, let the man go, and backed towards the dressing-table. He was glad to sit on the stool. The other had small, bright blue eyes, and was badly frightened. He kept licking his lips, and drew attention to their thinness; he could look vicious. He darted furtive glances towards the window and to the door, which might mean that he expected someone to come to his rescue. There was no sound in the house.

The housebreaker sat up slowly, rubbing his right wrist, still licking his lips. Martin stood up, and the man cringed away.

" Scared? " asked Martin.

His lips were dry, and his voice sounded hoarse, but his face gave nothing away. He stood over the man, and

67

then suddenly jabbed at his chin. He judged the blow to a nicety; the man's head jolted back and he flopped down and lay still.

Martin turned his back on him, but kept an eye on the mirror. The little man didn't move. Martin went to the door and crept downstairs on tip-toe. All the rooms were empty. He made sure there was no one in the garden, went upstairs again, saw that his victim was still unconscious, and studied the street from the bedroom window. A small car was parked about fifty yards away; possibly this man had arrived in it, and had walked that fifty yards to make sure that he couldn't be heard approaching. If he had stepped from the front gate to the lawn, he could have come within two yards of the porch without making a sound; from there, it would have been easy to reach the front door. How had he managed, then?

Was it really easy to force a Yale lock?

He made sure that the man was still unconscious, and went downstairs to examine the front door. It was closed; and if it had been opened, it had been with a key. He went to the back; that door was still bolted on the inside, and none of the windows in any of the downstairs rooms was open; that made it virtually certain that the man had used a key.

Martin went upstairs; his victim was stirring, his eyes flickering. Martin lifted him, and felt his body stiffen, carried him to a small bedroom chair and dumped him into it, then sat on the side of the bed, and waited. The deed-box was on the floor, only a few inches from his feet. He gave the man time to recover his wits and become alive to fear, then spoke; this time he wasn't hoarse, and his lips didn't feel dry.

"Who gave you the key?"

The man didn't answer.

"Listen to me," said Martin softly. "We're here alone, and I'm in charge of the house, you're a burglar." He remembered that burglary was a crime committed during the hours of darkness, and didn't correct himself; but his lips quirked. "I can beat you up so that your own mother wouldn't recognise you, and the police would congratulate me. You'd better talk. Who gave you the key?"

The man said, "My—my boss."

Martin gulped; his father might have been tapping at the typewriter, using those words this very minute.

"Don't try to pull that one. Who is your boss?"

"Smart Rummy." The little man was beginning to sweat. "I work for Smart Rummy, mister, he sent me along to get that box. Told me where I'd find it, told me what to do, he——"

"Where did you expect to find it?"

"Under—under the floorboards up 'ere."

"Really? Why not the wardrobe? Whereabouts?"

"In that corner."

The man pointed, and Martin glanced round. The corner was empty, except for a small chair. The man seemed too scared to be lying.

"Go and turn up the carpet," ordered Martin.

The man stood up, and with reluctant obedience moved forward. It struck Martin that he was actually enjoying this; the thought made him grin. His expression must have seemed sinister to the little man, who flinched as he passed between Martin and the dressing-table; there was no room to keep out of reach. He passed Martin—and Martin shot out his hand and grabbed his arm, swinging him round.

"Don't!" he gasped.

"What's your name?"

"Garrett, mister, Tim Garrett. Lemme go!"

Martin let him go, and decided that the name was probably genuine; it had come out so promptly. In any case, that could be checked. Garrett went to the corner and down on his knees, glanced round nervously, then pulled at the corner of the carpet. Martin saw that it was tacked close to the walls, but the tacks in the corner came up easily, as if they had been pulled up quite recently. Garrett wasted no time.

" Go ahead," Martin ordered.

Garrett obeyed, almost eagerly.

Two floorboards had been cut and screwed down. The screws were missing from the holes. Garrett started to prise up one piece of board, then looked round for approval. Martin nodded, and stood up. There was a hole beneath the floorboards, amply large enough to take the deed-box. He thought he could tell what had happened, now. Gillian had known of the hiding-place and had managed to get the boards up, but the deed-box itself had beaten her. She had put it in the wardrobe, away from casual gaze, probably intending to try to open it again.

" Now put it all back," Martin said, and as Garrett moved, changed his mind. " No, wait a minute."

He went across, and Garrett, doubtless remembering that one savage blow, cringed back. Martin went down on one knee and felt inside the hole. Nothing else was hidden there.

Garrett was pressed back against the wall, looking more frightened than ever; that wouldn't do him any harm. Martin stood up—but as he did so, his right foot caught in the rolled-back carpet, and he lost his balance. It was only for a moment; but it was long enough for Garrett. Martin, watching the man closely, couldn't do a thing to stop him.

Garrett leapt at him, kicked at his face and missed, but caught his shoulder and sent him reeling back. Garrett rushed to the door and thudded down the stairs. He must have been in the hall by the time Martin had recovered his balance and picked himself up. A door opened—and slammed. Martin hesitated, then went slowly to the window.

The little man was running along the garden-path, making no effort now to keep silent. He went like the wind, and didn't look over his shoulder until he reached the gate. He looked at the front door, seemed reassured, but didn't slacken his pace. No one was in the quiet street. He reached the little car, got in and started the engine. He reversed at wild speed, and drove off while Martin was still trying to make up his mind what to do. Some men would have used that gun.

Martin brushed his hair back from his forehead, rubbed his shoulder gingerly, and turned round. The castle in the air, built of the answers he would have received from Garrett to questions already framed, collapsed about his ears. The noise wasn't exactly deafening.

It was a pity that the man had escaped, in one way; in another, Garrett might have been an embarrassment. One thing was beginning to show clearly: Pete Dunn had known that Garrett was coming, had sent Gillian away, to make sure that she wasn't hurt. He had probably known that Garrett had the gun and been sure that he would use it, if necessary.

That couldn't be guessing; the facts surely made it obvious.

He did not ask himself the inevitable questions, but went back to the bed, sat down and, rubbing his shoulder thoughtfully, looked at the box. It shouldn't be difficult to break open, with the right tools; there would surely be something downstairs which he could use. The girl had tried; Garrett had come simply to get it, because—if he could be believed—a certain Smart Rummy had sent him. Even if Smart Rummy were a purely imaginary creature, the importance of the contents of the deed-box remained. Otherwise, why had Gillian tried to open it, and why had the thief wanted it?

He picked it up, handling it carelessly because of the adhesive tape, and took it downstairs. He bolted the front door, to make sure that no one could get in so easily again, and then, grinning to himself, went round the house and latched all the downstairs windows and locked the doors of the rooms on the outside. He had access only to the kitchen and the hall. He went through

71

drawer after drawer in the kitchen until he found an open cardboard box, fitted into one drawer and containing an assortment of tools. There were pliers, two screwdrivers, a small hammer, a hacksaw, other oddments, and small boxes of nails and screws, some odd nuts and bolts, one or two spare electric plugs, and some fuse-wire. The most likely tool for the deed-box was the larger of the two screwdrivers. To use it successfully, he would have to ruin the box. He picked it up—and hesitated.

The police——

He flung caution to the winds, and attacked the lock vigorously.

It was fully five minutes, and he was sweating and infuriated, before the lock snapped open.

9   THE WASH-LEATHER BAG

MARTIN did not pull the lid back immediately, but backed away from the kitchen table and wiped the sweat off his forehead. For a few seconds he had been furious with the box; small wonder Gillian hadn't been able to get it open. His fingers ached from the pressure, and the handle of the screwdriver had made a ridge on the ball of his thumb. He eased his fingers slowly and painfully, while staring at the box. Then he wiped his forehead again, gripped the thing with one hand and flung the lid up.

A wash-leather bag lay on top of some papers.

There were many papers, and the box was almost full without the wash-leather bag, which was about the size of a large orange; it was a pale yellow in colour, and dirty at the neck and bottom. The neck was tied with cord, and there had once been a lead seal on it; the seal was broken.

He lifted the bag out, and pressed; it contained something soft and yielding.

The papers sprang up when he took the bag away; it must have been squashed pretty tightly. Most of the papers were tied round with red tape, all legal-looking documents. Martin did not study these at first, but tossed the bag into the air; it was probably the cause of most of the trouble. It wasn't heavy. He had a pretty good idea what was inside.

He untied the cords and opened the neck, and wasn't surprised to see cotton-wool. He pulled at this and it came away in small, fluffy pieces, so he dug his finger right inside, and prised the whole lot up. It came out, a small round ball which fell lightly on to the table. He picked at this, and touched something hard; he saw a glint and knew that his guess had been on the mark; this was a jewel bag.

The jewel was a diamond, the size of a pea-nut; a lovely thing which caught the rays of the sun and stabbed brilliant lights at his eyes. He put it aside and felt the cotton-wool again, found another stone and added it to the first. He was conscious of a rising tide of excitement as he put one after another in a little heap.

There were several diamonds, all about the same size. He had no idea of their value, but guessed that it must be considerable, running into many thousands of pounds. He whistled softly to himself as he pressed the cotton-wool, made sure that nothing else was there, and then stood back to look at the scintillating heap of precious stones.

He chuckled aloud.

Soon he decided that it wasn't so funny; these jewels were almost certainly stolen.

He made himself look at the papers. Most of them were copies of mortgage deeds. Raymond Dunn owned a dozen houses in the London suburbs, and each of them had been heavily mortgaged; Martin made a rough total of the amounts involved; nearly twenty thousand pounds. Apparently the money had been paid to him during the past three years—and downstairs, his writing-table was crammed with letters from creditors, all for small amounts. In spite of having got his hands on money like this, he'd left his grocery, gas, and electricity bills unpaid, and hadn't even paid the rates of the house he lived in.

This was also mortgaged, for two thousand five hundred pounds.

There was nothing else.

Martin sat on a corner of the table and picked up one diamond; it dazzled him. He'd never seen a larger, anywhere; it could have made most of the diamonds in rings on show in jewellers' shops look small. Whenever he moved it, molten fire seemed to spring from it; the tiny facets each seemed to give off a different colour.

He had no proof that they were stolen, but had a pretty good idea. If he kept these from the police, he could expect to land himself in trouble. He had no excuse at all for saying nothing about them, yet reluctance to go to the police remained. So much was at stake—Pete's part, for instance. Had Pete known what would be found in the deed-box? Had Pete warned Gillian to leave so that the thief could come in and take these for the asking? Had Pete known of the hiding-place under the floorboards, and so told Smart Rummy where to find them?

He could go on asking a lot of equally ridiculous questions.

One of the most significant things was that Garrett had let himself in with a key. Where had he obtained it? From Pete? There was no reason to believe that Pete had a key of his brother's house. From Raymond? There was fairly strong evidence that Raymond Dunn had been kept away against his will; he might be a prisoner, and the key could easily have been taken from him.

The immediate problem was—what to do?

If he could put the jewels in a safe place, where there was no risk of their being stolen, he could satisfy his conscience, do no harm to anyone, and escape the worst consequences if the story eventually had to be told to the police. What could be considered a safe place? No one else must know about them; he was the only repository of that secret.

He couldn't carry them about with him.

His father's house?

He broke into a chuckle, but dismissed the idea; he certainly couldn't use his home as a hiding-place for precious stones that had almost certainly been stolen. The flat? Once Garrett and the man Smart Rummy, if he existed, had identified him, the flat would probably

75

be searched. The diamonds must be put somewhere quite safe, where no one would suspect. Was he asking for the impossible?

A bank or a safe deposit?

It was so easy to overlook the obvious, and one or the other was the obvious place. There wasn't likely to be a safe deposit in Guildford, but there was a branch of his bank. He glanced at his watch; it was a quarter to two. He hurried out and unlocked the lounge door, telephoned his bank manager and asked him to inform the manager of the Guildford branch of the Midclay Bank, Limited, that he was going to take a small packet there, for safe keeping. His bank manager could not have been more affable.

He called the local exchange, and an operator obligingly gave him the number of a taxi-rank. While waiting, he took the tape off his fingers, and wrapped it in a piece of newspaper which he put in his pocket. Twenty minutes later he left 17 Nye Road, and he was near the bank when he remembered Barbara's hand-bag; it was still on the chair where he had left it. He stifled the temptation to go back for it; rejected the thought that there was need for going through it. He might regret that, one day; in any case, he would almost certainly be back before Richard and Barbara. He grinned at this form of self-deception, made the arrangements with the bank, who accepted a large sealed envelope without knowing what was in it; he had to sign across the seal. Relieved, and feeling that it was completely out of danger, he left the bank, tucking the receipt into his pocket, and strolled towards the clock.

He was hungry.

He turned the corner towards Betty's, where they would probably serve a good lunch, late though it was, and then stopped abruptly. He had overlooked an elementary possibility; that he had been watched at Nye Road and followed. He'd noticed no car; but surely Garrett would have gone to the nearest telephone to

76

report what had happened; and Smart Rummy would probably have decided to watch him, because he knew what was in the deed-box.

He stood at the corner for a few moments, noticed no one suspicious, and then asked himself how he could possibly judge a "suspicious" character. The least likely man—or woman—might be involved. He kept a clear mind-picture of everyone who was near at hand— there were comparatively few—and then went to Betty's.

The luncheon was excellent.

No one waited outside the café while he was inside, and no one followed him from the place; he could at least be sure of that. Garrett had probably rushed as far from Guildford as he could get, had probably been here alone, and "Smart" probably lived in London. They would guess that he had the diamonds; they couldn't possibly . guess where he had taken them.

They would probably suspect that he'd gone to the police; that would do them good.

He chuckled again as he asked a policeman where he could find a taxi; the policeman obviously wondered what caused him so much amusement.

It was twenty minutes past three when he reached Number 17 Nye Road. Two women, each pushing a pram, were walking towards him as he paid off the taxi. An elderly man was clipping a box-hedge in his front garden; it had been lucky that no one had been about when Garrett had taken to his heels. He let himself in, went briskly into the lounge, and then remembered that he must be cautious.

He had warned anyone who might be lurking here that he'd returned; couldn't have warned them more effectively by calling out to say so. He went through the house, found no indication that anyone else had been here, but was annoyed to find that he had left the broken deed-box and the papers on the kitchen-table. His father would tell him that he made a poor imitation of the Prince—a fictitious hero of remarkable resource. He took the box and the documents up to the bedroom, tucked them into the hole in the floor, and put the carpet back into position.

Now he could relax.

Richard and Barbara might be back at any time, and——

The hand-bag!

He thought of it as he thought of the girl—when he was half-way down the stairs. He went into the lounge, and it lay where he had tossed it, a large bag as hand-bags went, somehow unmistakably Barbara Marrison's. That was fancy, but it suited her.

She had been extremely well dressed, which probably meant that she had money.

What did she want from Pete?

What had Pete intended to tell her?

He filled his pipe and called himself a fool. He had cheerfully and recklessly taken thousands of pounds' worth of jewels which didn't belong to him and signed his name for them; he had smashed that deed-box; he had made a search of a house, which was certainly a criminal offence; and here he was, having an attack of conscience over opening a hand-bag. The girl need never know that he'd looked inside.

He picked up the bag.

Unbidden, he saw a picture of her, as she had laughed when he had joked with Richard. He felt heavy-hearted, and remembered how flat he had been after they had gone. Then, almost savagely, he opened the bag.

There were three compartments inside; the usual things a woman would carry. A mirror fitted into a little pocket, with a comb; there was a green handkerchief and a red one, powder compact, lipstick, a pair of nail scissors and a nail file, two letters addressed to Miss Barbara Marrison, 27 Leyton Court, Mayfair, W.1. He knew that block of flats; while it wasn't the most exclusive, anyone who lived at Leyton Court had a reasonably good income. He knew that to do the job

78

thoroughly he should open the letters. Both were addressed by hand, and he thought a man had written each; not the same man.

He put them aside.

There was a purse, a note-case with seven or eight pound notes in it, some keys on a small ring, and a fold of paper. The paper was shiny and creased, she had obviously carried it about with her for some time. He took that out, and opened it without compunction, not having the slightest idea what he would find.

It was good-quality art paper, folded several times, and as he unfolded it he saw that something, not words, was printed on the inside. They were pictures of a kind, and beneath each were some figures. Dotted lines ran beneath each " picture " and along one side; at the ends of the lines were tiny arrows, and in the middle, tiny figures—in millimetres. He saw all this as the truth about the " pictures " dawned on him.

There were seven altogether; drawings of diamonds giving the dimensions and the weight, in carats. At the foot of the sheet of paper, which was octavo in size, were three words: *The Rossmore Diamonds*. Beneath that, the paper had been torn neatly; there had been more printing, but he couldn't guess what.

He looked at the gaping green bag.

" I wonder what you could tell us, Barbara," he said heavily.

He glanced out of the window as he spoke—and as he did so, the nose of the Blond Beauty came into sight.

MARTIN folded the sheet of paper to its original size, put it back with the letters, pushed everything else into the bag, and hoped that Barbara would not remember exactly how each had been placed. He closed the bag and put it back on the table where he had found it. He heard the car horn; it had a two-tone braying sound, and Richard amused himself with playing a tune on it. Martin went to the door and had it open by the time the others came along the path.

Barbara was a step ahead of Richard, who waved cheerfully; but judging from Barbara's expression, they'd had no luck.

" Found him? " Martin called, as they drew nearer.

" No trace," Richard said.

Barbara drew up, and put out a hand.

" Have you any news? "

" Not that you'd call news, but there's been a little excitement."

Martin gave his lazy grin, and refused to explain as he went into the lounge. He appeared to be interested mostly in Richard, but didn't miss the way Barbara's gaze went to her bag; or the relief in her eyes when she saw that it was where she had left it. When she looked at him, he thought there was both doubt and questioning in her eyes.

" We will now be told all about the excitement," said Richard.

" Thief," announced Martin.

Barbara cried, " No! "

Richard's eyes glistened.

"You lucky dog, it would happen to you. Where is he?"

" Flown."

Richard looked at him in disbelief.

" You mean you actually had a thief here, and let him *go*? " He sank into a chair. " I knew it was the wrong way round. You ought to have gone Pete-hunting, I ought to have stayed here. My dear chap, what happened? Was he a colossus, or did he have a gun or something, or——"

" He had a gun."

Richard stopped in the middle of a word, and sank farther back into his chair. Without speaking, Barbara went across to another chair and sat on the arm. She was close to the table, and stretched across and picked up her hand-bag; it was impossible to be sure, but she seemed to do that almost too casually.

" I can't bear it," Richard said. " Did he shoot? "

" I discouraged him."

Martin took the automatic out of his pocket, and tossed it into the air.

" Here, be careful with that, it might be loaded! " Richard cried in alarm. " Do you mean—oh, no." He became superior. " I'm not falling for that one at my time of life. Where did you get the gun? Whistled up a friend of yours, I suppose. I didn't know you had so many friends."

" You don't have to believe me."

" But—but if you disarmed him, how did he get away? "

" I tripped and he ran," said Martin lazily, and smiled at Barbara, who was listening intently, and nursing her bag. " His name was Garrett."

Barbara's hands tightened on the bag.

" So you were on speaking terms," said Richard dryly. " On the whole, not good, Scoop. I'll have to report you to the Maestro. The Prince would have bound the villain hand and foot and stuffed a gag in his mouth and put him in the attic or down a well or somewhere. Then he would have called on his trusty aide, say me, and given the said aide the opportunity of making him

81

cough up the ugly story. The name of his boss, and such-like. What was he like?"

"Just a little man, scared stiff."

"As you had the gun, I don't blame him. Barbara, what do you think of this ridiculous stewardship? We leave him here for a few hours, and he gets into trouble with armed thugs. We mustn't leave him alone again. What was the squirt after?"

"I wish I knew," said Martin ruefully.

He glanced at Barbara; was it imagination, or did she seem relieved to hear that he didn't know?

"He went into the bedroom, and I was in the bathroom. I caught him turning up the corner of a carpet, and after he'd gone, investigated." The ease of the invention surprised him. "There's a hole in the floor, a busted deed-box with some mortgage documents in it, but nothing else."

Barbara said sharply, "Are you sure?"

"Go and look for yourself," suggested Martin.

"Me, too," said Richard. "Until I see the visual evidence, I reject the whole story. Coming, Bar?"

So he had shortened "Barbara"! She shook her head, and he went out quickly, humming to himself as he hurried up the stairs. Barbara sat on the arm of the chair, her legs crossed, her hands relaxed, now, but still nursing the bag. Was it possible that she hadn't told Richard that she had left it behind? She seemed to be thinking nothing of the bag as she looked at Martin. The questions were in her eyes; and the doubts. The weight of anxiety was on her again, yet he recalled that moment of laughter, and the beauty of her then. He felt the flatness which had come to him when she had left; he did not like to think that she was involved. He could ask her, flat out.

"Did the man tell you anything else?" she asked.

"No, he wasn't here long," Martin chuckled. "I'm a mug at this game, I ought to have made sure that he couldn't get away. I'm sorry you had no luck, but Pete——"

"Have you told the police?"

That mattered to her; and he took it for granted that she didn't want the answer to be yes.

" No."

She didn't show any relief.

" Why not? "

" Call it a kind of misguided loyalty to Pete," he said lightly. " I'd like to know a bit more about it before the police come in. We can't leave it too long, but this chap Garrett did no great harm, he didn't get away with anything, and I don't think he'll come again in a hurry. I fancy what he wanted was in the deed-box, and someone else had stolen it before him. Someone without a key. I confess it's a complete mystery, but a word with Pete might clear a lot of it up. You don't know anything about it, do you ? "

That question came so casually, she couldn't possibly be expecting it. She was startled, but didn't appear to be annoyed. Then she smiled and reminded him of the picture he had so clearly in his mind. She had not only beauty but also the look of goodness, which showed in her eyes, touched now with merriment. The quick change of expression showed the mobility of her features —and her smile curved her lips and gave a hint of dimples. Her eyes danced, too.

" I do not! " she said.

Martin forced himself to ask bluntly:

" What did Pete have to tell you? "

" I haven't seen him, so I don't know."

She was almost too casual about that, and less amused; she changed so quickly.

" What kind of thing was it? Why are you so anxious to see him? "

" It's a personal matter," she said firmly. The smile had faded, he thought that she was nervous lest he pressed the questions too far. " I'm sorry, there's nothing I can tell you about it. Certainly not until I've seen Pete, it's largely up to him." She stood up, still clutching her hand-bag. " What are you going to do next? "

83

Richard, coming down the stairs, heard the question.

" Go and see Gillian," he said. " Under the paternal influence of the Maestro, she may have mellowed a bit, and be ready to tell us all about the villainy of her husband. Nasty piece of work, our Raymond, I've never felt so sorry for Pete. Bar, believe it or not, it's there. Pieces cut out of the floorboards to make a hiding-place, a lock busted by an amateur "—he grinned at Martin— " anyone could see that the chap concerned was ham-handed. No sign of a struggle, though, if it weren't for the gun I'd say that Martin had made up this story of a visitor just to impress us. You'll come with us to Dorset, won't you? "

He didn't change the tone of his voice; he hadn't spoken to Martin about the invitation; he was coolly inviting her to join Gillian, at his father's house. His right eyelid flickered as he spoke, in silent request to Martin not to spoil the effect of the question. Barbara didn't answer.

" If we're going to find Pete, we'll get the vital clue from Gillian," Richard said, dropping his voice and almost hissing the words. " You want to find him as much as I do. Why not throw in your lot with us, as it were? There's plenty of room in old Blond Beauty."

" I'd like to find Pete," she said, " but I can't stay away from London to-night. I'm sorry, I'd love to come."

" Change your mind. Martin's nothing like the dull stick he seems to be, you ought to hear him singing after the third pint of beer or the second whisky-and-soda! Come with us in Pete's place, until we find Pete. Even then there'll be room for you. And——"

" I wish I could." Barbara's tone was final. " It just isn't possible. If you'll let me have your address for to-night, I can tell you if I hear from Pete. I live at Leyton Court, W.1—Number 27."

" Make a note of that, Sergeant Martin," Richard said. " With luck, we'll be at Nairn Lodge, Lichen Abbas, Dorset. Just north of Dorchester. Telephone, Lichen

Abbas three-three. Don't blame us for the name, a Scotsman built it. Creeper-clad and a Georgian gem, plenty of room, and we'd always be glad to see you. If you call and we're not there, present yourself as a friend of Martin's. You will not then be suspected of being a scarlet woman." He clapped his hands above the easy ripple of nonsense. " Sure you won't come with us? "

" Yes."

" Far be it from me to tell a lady that it's time she got a move on," said Richard, " but we have to take you into Guildford to pick up your car and then hit the great highway. It'll take us four hours or more, and we shan't be away until after five. You haven't any crazy notion of staying here, have you, Martin? "

" I don't think so."

" Sense percolates slowly," Richard said.

He was in high spirits, without any apparent reason.

" On the other hand, I don't know that we ought to go without telling the police what happened," Martin said.

He appeared to be serious about these second thoughts, and watched Barbara closely. She most certainly did not want the police to be consulted, but she didn't say so.

" Forget it, until we've consulted the Maestro," Richard said. " A few hours won't make any difference. As I said before, Gillian might be in a mood to tell us all, and then the whole thing would be neatly explained. Barbara, did I think to ask if you'd come to Nairn Lodge with us? "

Barbara laughed, unexpectedly. Would she be able to laugh so easily and so freely if she really had anything on her conscience?

. . . . .

" Now there is a nice little car and as pretty a driver as I've ever seen," said Richard, watching Barbara Marrison without trying to keep the admiration out of his eyes. " Quite a girl, Scoop. I wouldn't mind getting to know her. She certainly knows how to handle that green whippet, too."

85

Barbara, at the wheel of a green M.G. sports car, slid through a congestion of traffic towards the London Road. She didn't look back. The deep note of the engine was louder than any others nearby, Martin imagined that he could pick it out. He remembered the way she had dropped her hand-bag carelessly on to the seat next to her; could imagine that he could still feel the firm clasp of her hand.

" Oh, well," Richard said. " It would have been fun if she'd come. Thanks for the poker face."

" Why did you ask her? "

" Because I've come to the conclusion that our Barbara isn't all she seems," said Richard, and grinned. Martin, at the wheel of Blond Beauty, started the engine. " Item —when I crashed in with ' The man must be at death's door ' she took it literally—remember? "

Martin nodded; and also remembered that Richard's mind was as sharp as a needle, although he seldom allowed others to realise it.

" You're improving! Also, she left her hand-bag behind. She didn't say anything about it, but I saw her looking round, on the outskirts of London, for the usual refresher of face-powdering and lip-sticking and all that kind of thing. She just did without it. When she came back, she sidled across to the bag and picked it up and didn't say a word about having left it. Now, why? If that bag had innocuous contents, would she care? " He lit a cigarette with some difficulty, because the wind cut in through the open window, and went on with a laugh in his voice: " If I'd stayed behind instead of you, I'd have gone through that bag and made a list of the contents. You didn't, by any chance, did you? "

" Yes."

" What? "

Richard was shrill.

" All I found that I didn't expect to find was a printed list of some jewels. The Rossmore Diamonds. It doesn't

86

mean a thing. Everything else was about what you'd expect. There were a couple of letters, but——"

Richard groaned.

" You were too much of a gentleman to look through them. Idiot child. The whole dark mystery might have been solved if you'd read and digested the contents. Oh, well, you didn't do so badly. I laid it on thick that Gillian might have the secret, in the hope that it would make Barbara come with us—and if she'd come, wouldn't we have known that she was in this up to the neck? "

" Yes, wouldn't we," said Martin, gruffly.

He ought to have read those letters; they probably had nothing to do with the mystery, but he should have read them; Richard had made him feel a fool.

" By the way," asked Richard, " what did you find in the deed-box? The jewels? "

MARTIN could deny it; Richard wouldn't believe him if he did. He stared straight ahead, concentrating on the road, but knew that Richard was grinning, his eyes bright and merry, the cigarette drooping from his lips. He could picture the careless good looks, the curly hair just a little untidy, the negligent way in which Richard sat back in his seat. His legs were stretched out, and the creases in his flannels were perfect. He chuckled.

"This is a time when your theory of absolute truthfulness or saying nothing comes unstuck. I had a good look at that deed-box. Only someone as ham-handed as you could have made such a mess of it. You've never been a handy-man. I could imagine you feeling you could throw the thing out of the window, before the lock broke. Were the jewels in it?"

"Yes."

Richard said: "Well, well! Where have you hidden the fortune?"

"It's at a bank."

Martin didn't say what bank.

"You moved fast," approved Richard. "I wouldn't have thought twice about it, but you were so poker-faced I knew you were hiding something from our Barbara, and probably had quixotic notions about not letting me know that there were stolen jools about."

"Why say stolen?"

"I'd say it, even if I didn't know for sure. I do know. If you read the papers occasionally, instead of drawing your pretty drawings for advertisements and making people laugh—occasionally!—you'd know, also. The Rossmore Diamonds were stolen about five months ago from the safe of the Earl of Rossmore. There was quite a song and dance, and—I apologise! You were in Paris, you went over to have a look at the French advertising agencies. I remember the time, because I had a few friends at the flat one night, and one of the floosies had a diamond about as big as a peanut for an engagement ring. We decided that she'd stolen it. She was most indignant, so I didn't ask her again. January. I don't remember much about the details, except that it was a daring job, from Rossmore's London flat."

Martin caught up with a milk-lorry, and had to slow down behind it to let approaching cars pass.

" Quite sure, Skip? "

" Oh, yes. I'm trying to remember the value. We can find that when we want to, of course, but it was somewhere in the region of twenty-five thousand pounds, that's the headline figure that jogs about in front of my mind. How shall we share the spoils? Two-thirds to you, one to me? "

The laughter was deep in his voice.

" You can have your share when you've earned it," Martin said dryly. " Well, this makes it a police job."

" Meaning, they'll know that you know the jewels were stolen? Why? You took a peek into Barbara's hand-bag, otherwise I could have crooned Rossmore all day long and you wouldn't have guessed a thing. No one knows you took that peek. You are still a man of unblemished reputation." Richard's chuckle was almost a gurgle. " When Dad knows about this, he'll be tickled pink. He probably won't believe a word of it, and will say we're stringing him along. I wonder what kind of reception Gillian got."

" They'll look after her, all right."

" Oh, yes."

They went on for several minutes, and Martin didn't take his eyes off the road. He was concentrating on all Richard had said, and had recovered from the defeat he'd

89

suffered; if he'd acted well, he need not have told the truth about the diamonds.

"Bit glum, Scoop, aren't you?" Richard asked suddenly. "It doesn't greatly matter that you've been caught out, I won't split. Have a cigarette?"

"No, thanks." Martin glanced at the dashboard clock. "It's half-past five, and we've a hundred and twenty miles to go, I'd better get a move on."

"Like me to drive?"

"Later."

"I know, I know. When we get to the nasty twisting bits of road in rural Dorset," scoffed Richard. "We'll just about make it before dark, if we don't have a puncture or break a big-end or something. You must agree that Percy Mellor's boasts for the Beauty are standing up pretty well."

"So far," said Martin, ominously.

.   .   .   .   .

An hour later, between Basingstoke and Winchester, Martin felt the steering-wheel getting wobbly. He slowed down and pulled up at the side of the road. He didn't speak. Richard glanced at him, shook his head sadly, and buried his face in his hands. Then, without a word, he got out and walked round the car. He spent most time at the front, came back, leaned against Martin's window, and said sadly:

"Curse Percy Mellor. We have a flat."

"Which one?"

"Does it matter? Nearside front. The tyre looks perfect, too."

"The inner tubes are probably perished," said Martin. "So now you have to change the wheel. Take your coat off."

"We could flag a car and I could nip along to the nearest garage——"

"Oh, no. If anyone goes along to the nearest garage, I shall. I'd much rather watch you change that wheel," said Martin, with a glint in his eyes. "It's a pleasure I've been awaiting for a long time. Remember your proud boast? Quote 'If anything goes wrong, I'll do everything.' Unquote."

" Sadist," groaned Richard. " Oh, well. What tools do we want? Jack—brrh! I don't know where to fix the jack on this monster. Brace, or whatever they call it —I wonder where they keep the tools? "

" In the back."

" Sure? "

" I haven't looked, but it's usual on Buicks."

" All right," said Richard. He took the keys and went dejectedly to the back of the car. The large boot had not yet been opened. He fiddled for a few minutes, and then, " It won't open."

" I've heard that kind of story before," said Martin. " Try the key."

" What do you think I'm trying? It won't fit." The sound of keys came, then a shaking; and there was no result. He came towards the front as Martin climbed down. " No fooling, old chap, the key just won't fit. I took it for granted that it would be the same key for the boot as for the doors."

Martin tried; the door wouldn't budge.

" When I see Percy——" began Richard.

" That will be in about three weeks' time." Martin stood back and considered. " It's just possible that——"

" Hold it! " cried Richard, peering along the road to Winchester. " What's that coming along? Can it be——" He paused, and then laughed with sheer delight. " It is, it's a breakdown lorry! "

He stepped into the road and waved, and the small breakdown van slowed down. He grinned at the driver, who grinned back, spontaneously.

Twenty-five minutes after they had stopped they were on the road again.

" And remember, I paid," said Richard righteously. " We must slip into a garage in the morning and get a key for that luggage-boot. Wouldn't do to run far without being able to get at the tools, would it? "

"Apparently not," Martin said heavily.

"Shall I drive?"

"Not if you think you're going to make up for lost time."

"Nothing over a hundred miles an hour," Richard promised earnestly. He took the wheel, and they started off. Not far along was a garage, and he slowed down. "Better fill up with petrol, hadn't we? They might have a spare key for that boot, too." He swung off the road, and a plump, middle-aged man came forward to serve them, with a boy in attendance.

The garage stood back from the road, and on one side was protected by a row of trees. Drivers coming from London could see the garage sign but not the garage itself. As the boy put in the petrol the plump man went to look for some spare keys, and Richard and Martin stood at the side of the car, Richard jingling coins in his pocket, Martin drawing comfortingly at his pipe. Richard chuckled suddenly.

"No one would think you'd been up to such fancy tricks this afternoon, my boy. On the whole, I think you'll make a better crook than I. I——"

He stopped abruptly.

Martin, also looking towards the road, saw a new Armstrong-Siddeley pass, beautifully lined, chocolate in colour. They also saw the woman at the wheel and the man by her side. They didn't notice much about the man, they were interested chiefly in the fact that Barbara Marrison was on the same road.

.   .   .   .   .

Barbara had not looked round; the trees had probably hidden the cream car from her until she had passed it; she may not have noticed it, even then. They watched the car out of sight without saying a word.

"Well, well," breathed Richard. "We always said she was a woman of mystery, didn't we? Not bad! She rejects our kind offer, slips back to town, changes her car and—but she hasn't had time to slip back to town, has she? Allowing for the hold-up, say half an hour, she's no more than five or ten minutes behind us. It would have taken her three-quarters of an hour to get to town, the same back. So she had this gent and the Armstrong-Siddeley tucked away in Guildford. My, my! Aren't women deceitful? "

The plump man heard the last words of this, and smiled to himself.

" I'm sorry, but I haven't a key that will fit," he said. " You might get one in Winchester, but most of the big garages will be shut by now."

" Oh. Thanks. Pity," Richard said. " We'll get to Blandford in time for dinner, with luck," he added to Martin, " and after that it won't be long."

He took the wheel again, and for the next three-quarters of an hour drove the Buick almost as fast as she would go. The car went beautifully, and Richard seemed to be thoroughly enjoying himself. Neither of them spoke again of the fact that Barbara Marrison had passed them on the road, and was almost certainly heading for Lichen Abbas.

They stopped at the Crown Hotel in the sleepy market town of Blandford, dined well if hurriedly, and were on the road again just before nine o'clock. It would take them nearly an hour to reach the little village of Lichen Abbas; it was twenty miles away, and the road was winding and narrow; in the half-light even Richard would not take chances. Once they were off the main road, and driving between tall hedges, thick with leaves, he switched on the headlights. These lit up the dusk with a silvery brightness, shone on the rabbits which sped across the road, gave plenty of warning to the few cyclists and the occasional car which came towards them.

" Steady just here," Martin said suddenly.

They were approaching a sharp corner, with a steep hill beyond it and then an acute S bend. Tall trees grew in a copse, through which the road was cut; it was familiar to anyone who used the road—a notorious danger

spot. Richard slowed down to twenty, swung the wheel
—and jammed on the brakes.

A motor cyclist was on the road immediately in front
of them—off his machine, which lay on its side. The
headlights shone on the man's face and crash helmet, on
the glittering chromium of the machine. He raised his
hands and jumped, as if for safety. He need not have
worried; they pulled up ten yards away.

" Nice of you to remember," Richard said. " Looks as
if he's had a spill. Pity we can't offer tools! "

The motor cyclist was coming towards them now.

" Anything we can do? " Richard asked.

" Sure." The man sounded eager, as he drew up.
" Sorry if I give you a n'eart attack. Came off five
minutes ago, only just started to sit up and take notice
again." His smile looked nervous. " I don't know what
happened, I think there must have been something in the
road that——"

He broke off.

Martin exclaimed, " The devil you do! Drive on,
Skip! "

He leaned forward, buffeted the motor cyclist in the face
and sent him sprawling backwards.

" Drive on! "

Richard started the engine and let in the clutch,
bewildered but obeying the urgent command.

It was too late. Two men ran from the copse, one from
each side. The first passed the motor cyclist; there was
sufficient light to show the gun in his hand.

12

RICHARD stepped on the accelerator as a man smacked a blow at his chin. His foot slipped and the engine stalled. Martin shot out a hand towards the other door, but it opened before he touched it, and a man stood a few feet away, covering him with a gun.

There was more light that side of the road, for the background of trees was not so thick. This man was Garrett.

" Stay put," Garrett ordered.

" That goes for you," a man said from the other side.

Richard had straightened up, and was opening his door. He ignored the order, pushed the door back, and missed the man by inches. He scrambled out. One man ran at him, and Martin saw the confusion of movement and heard the sounds of a scuffle. A man fell, and it wasn't Richard.

A shot rang out.

The sound was loud and sharp in the evening quiet; and carried with it an undertone of horror.

There was no cry of pain.

Martin held his breath and watched Richard, who stood quite still, hair tousled, hands clenched by his side. The man who had fired the shot moved slowly forward, another went behind Richard and gripped his right arm, forcing it behind him in a hammer-lock.

" Next time I'll hit you," said the man who had fired.

Martin sat back in his seat, limp with relief. He could no longer see Richard's face, but knew that his brother was being forced to the side of the road. The man who had spoken came round to his side of the car, and Garrett, who was keeping his distance in spite of the gun in his hand, said harshly:

" That's him."

" Are you sure? "

" I wouldn't forget him in a month of Sundays."

" All right." The other had a calm, authoritative voice; there was no coarseness in it, and he seemed not only to be in command but also in control of the situation. " Get out, Fane," he ordered.

Martin stayed where he was.

" Let me put a bullet in him," Garrett growled.

" Get out, Fane," repeated the other man. He sounded older; he wore a hat and was dressed in a light-grey suit, and it was impossible to see his face clearly. " It won't help if you're stubborn. I don't want to hurt you, I only want the diamonds."

" *I'd* hurt him," said Garrett.

" Be quiet. Come on, Fane."

If Martin sat there much longer, he would probably be shot. He was prepared to believe that they wanted only the diamonds; there couldn't be any other reason for holding them up on the road. With a sickening sense of dismay he remembered that Barbara Marrison had come along this road; he had to accept the possibility that she was a party to this.

He shifted towards the door.

" Watch him," Garrett warned.

As he climbed out Martin sensed the hatred in the man's voice.

Something hard, in Martin's pocket, knocked against the side of the car: the gun he had taken from Garrett. A moment earlier he might have found a use for it, but there wouldn't be much chance now. He felt a sickening sense of futility as he stood upright, nearly a head taller than either of the others. Garrett kept some distance off —a menacing figure; nothing would give him more pleasure than to use his automatic. The man in grey leaned inside the Buick and switched off the lights.

" Now——" he began.

" Skip! " called Martin. " You all right? "

" I could be worse," Richard called. " Break their ruddy necks."

" All in good time," Martin called; and grinned.

The calm-voiced man said quietly: " This isn't funny, Fane, don't try any more back-chat. Where are the diamonds? "

" What diamonds? "

" I told you——" began Garrett.

" You can have a go at him if he doesn't change his tune," said the man in grey; and obviously he meant it. " We've been back to the house, and found the deed-box, broken open. You were the only man with a chance to do that—you or your brother, and you're more likely. I've told you, you won't get hurt if you hand the diamonds over."

" I don't know what you're talking about."

The man in grey said harshly: " Don't stall. If you waste time, I'll let Garrett put a bullet in your guts. He's longing to do just that."

" Take it easy, Scoop," Richard called from the other side of the road, and a man growled something which Martin didn't hear. The few moments of respite had helped. The success of the hold-up would depend on speed; this was a lonely country road, but there would be some traffic, the man in grey and his men couldn't stay for long. He knew it, and it showed in the edginess of his voice.

" Fane! I'll give you one more chance."

" Oh, to hell with you," growled Martin, and dug his right hand into his pocket.

The grey-clad man probably realised his mistake then. He darted forward and blocked Garrett's view. Martin felt the gun, and it was the right way round. He had no time to take it out, raised it against his coat and fired. The roar was muffled and there was no flame, just a smell of burning. The man in grey gasped and backed away.

97

Garrett fired.

Martin, knowing that was inevitable, leapt to one side; he felt nothing. He turned, snatching the gun out of his pocket. Two shots rang out, simultaneously. He felt pain pluck at his left forearm, and heard Garrett cry out. Next came a metallic thud, and he knew the other's gun had fallen. He sprang at the man in grey, who was still reeling back and had no gun.

Garrett turned and ran.

The man in grey shot out a leg and kicked Martin in the stomach.

It hurt much more than the wound in the arm. Martin pulled up short and lost control of his muscles. That wasn't for long, but in the unending minute, he knew that he was completely at the mercy of any man who had a gun. He heard confused sounds, of shouting—and of thudding footsteps. He heard a louder shout, and then a man rushed towards him.

" Scoop——"

" Gun," gasped Martin. " On ground. No—here! "

Richard snatched the gun from his weak grasp and fired blindly towards men who were running away. There were three of them, all vague figures against the darkness of the copse. Another man passed, running wildly; and the motor cycle, which had been moved, started up. Martin swung round as Richard fired; a bullet struck metal. The man on the machine leapt off and started to run in the wake of the others.

Richard growled, " I'd shoot every ruddy tyke! "

He broke into a run.

" Skip! " cried Martin. " Skip! "

Richard hesitated and lost precious yards. The footsteps sounded much farther away, and the men had disappeared in the gloom. The engine of a car started up.

" Hold it," Martin said, more easily. " I'm all right. Don't want to take a corpse home, it wouldn't be welcome."

Richard didn't speak.

Martin straightened up and rubbed his stomach, gingerly; he would know all about that kick for some time, but pain wasn't important. They'd put four men to flight; the men's car was moving away at speed now, in top gear. They saw its headlights through the trees. That and the sound faded, and silence fell upon the copse and the road. Martin moved towards the Buick, and leaned on it heavily, while Richard went to the motor cycle, calling:

" Lend a hand, will you? "

Martin didn't move. Richard lifted one end of the machine and dragged it into the side of the road, then approached the car. Martin was holding his left arm tightly; blood had trickled down the sleeve and spread over the back of his hand.

" What——" began Richard.

" It's only a scratch."

" Let me see."

Richard took Martin's other arm and led him towards the front of the car, then went back and switched on the headlights. Martin shrugged off his coat. The wound looked bad, but probably wasn't serious; it had taken out a little groove of flesh. His short sleeve was already soaked with blood, which was dripping on to the road. Richard pulled a handkerchief from his pocket, twisted it round the wounded arm above the elbow, then stuck a fountain-pen through the knot and twisted, making a rough tourniquet which would probably serve its purpose.

No one came near.

Richard took out another handkerchief, mopped up the blood, and peered at the wound.

The bleeding had stopped completely. He tied the second handkerchief lightly round the wound and helped Martin to put his coat on again, leaving the left arm out of its sleeve.

" Mind if I drive? " asked Richard.

Martin found himself grinning.

He was glad to sit down; was glad of the nip of whisky

which Richard gave him from a pocket flask. Then Martin remembered the gun he had knocked or shot out of Garrett's hand. Richard went back, found it, and came hurrying to the car. They didn't speak as he started off again. This time he didn't take much care, but drove at speed.

"We ought to get that wound washed," Richard said.

"Wait until we get home."

For the first few miles Martin half-expected another hold-up. There was none. They passed through a small village, and the headlights shone on the windows of the cottages and the wicket gate of the church; the Norman tower showed square and squat against the sky, which was brighter to the west in the afterglow. A constable was standing by the side of a cottage, farther along, leaning on his bicycle.

"Going to tell him?" Richard asked.

"Leave it."

"They'll take it for granted we told the police," said Richard. "I don't think we'll have any more trouble to-night." He laughed; it was an explosive, high-pitched sound. "I thought we'd a single ticket to Kingdom Come. Congratulations."

"Mutual."

"We've hit something," Richard said. "I don't mean in the road! I mean, Pete's led us into a pretty do. I'd rejoice, but for one thing, I think."

"Barbara Marrison?"

"Yes."

"Pity," Martin said.

"Of course, we can't be sure that she knows anything about this," Richard tried to argue. "The more I think of it, the less likely it seems that she'd have anything to do with a mob like that. They're deadly. If you hadn't——"

"If we hadn't."

"Granted. If no one had lashed out, they would have shot us to get those diamonds. They took a hell of a chance—must have been pretty sure that we had them and equally sure that we shouldn't put up much of a fight. I suppose they thought you were carrying them about in your pocket." He paused, then added abruptly, " Think Raymond Dunn was mixed up with that mob? "

" It seems something like that," said Martin.

" Hm, yes."

Richard lapsed into silence, pausing only once to grope in the dashboard pocket for the flask and hand it to Martin. Martin refused it. Richard stopped the car and insisted on loosening the tourniquet, then tightened it again. The arm wasn't painful; Martin's stomach was much worse, and he felt sick. He leaned back and then forward, to try to ease the pains, and gradually they got better. Soon they passed familiar landmarks: a cottage on a corner, another small village, a larger one, where there were coloured lights outside a village hall and the sound of music. Beyond this, the road narrowed; there were only seven miles to go. Six miles on they would come to the village of Lichen Abbas, a huddle of thatched cottages, two or three larger houses, several farms, and a Norman church. Beyond, they would pass an old Roman burial ground, turn right, and find themselves at the foot of the drive leading to Nairn Lodge.

They passed through the village, and Richard asked:

" What's the time? That dashboard clock's stopped."

Martin studied his watch; the illuminated dial showed vaguely. They were near the gates of the drive before he was able to say:

" Just on ten."

" Everything considered, we haven't done so badly," said Richard, and there was a ghost of a laugh in his voice. " Unless the beggars are waiting on the drive, we've seen the end of them to-night. Gun at the ready? "

" Yes."

" I almost believe you." Richard paused, then went on less easily: " I hadn't thought of it before, but they might have a crack at the house. I should hate to lead

the Maestro and Mother into a show like this. I think
we ought to tell the police as soon as we get home, don't
you? "

" Yes. We're several hours too late."

" Pity," sighed Richard.

He turned into the drive. The gates were open, and
showed up white against the tall banks on either side.
These banks were wooded and planted with flowering
shrubs, all hidden now, but giving promise of the morning's beauty. Then the lights shone on the house itself, a
tall, square, graceful early Georgian building, with
wistaria climbing about the walls, white-painted shutters,
some of them closed, lights shining from tall windows.
They were nearing the house, and Richard swung right,
to turn towards the garage, when the porch light went on:
they had been heard. He was smiling, when the headlights fell on a car parked at the side of the house; there
was room for him to pass, but he didn't. He jammed on
the brakes and sent Martin shooting forward; and he
didn't apologise.

He sat, gaping.

Martin said in a curiously flat voice, " Well, we can't
say we aren't having a nice welcome."

The chocolate-coloured Armstrong-Siddeley, the one
in which Barbara Marrison had travelled, was facing
them.

13

RICHARD put on the hand-brake and leaned across and opened the door for Martin, who climbed out and looked grimly at the chocolate-coloured car. Heavy footsteps sounded on the gravel of the drive; not his mother's. She often came to the door to greet them, his father usually waited inside.

Another light went on, in a room at the side of the house, and fell upon the burly figure of Jonathan Fane as he came towards the car. He wore a cream-coloured linen coat, had a pipe at his mouth, and walked with a slight limp; Martin always noticed that when he had been away for a few weeks, but quickly became used to it. Richard came round from the other side, and none of them spoke; this was unusual constraint.

The light shone on Martin's arm, bent up beneath the coat, and with the sleeve hanging loose.

" Hallo, Scoop," said Jonathan Fane. " Hallo, Skip. You've been out-shining me, I gather. I've managed to write about it for thirty-odd years without getting mixed up in it! " The half-laughing note in his voice was reminiscent of Richard's, its depth was Martin's. " Arm bad? "

" Just a scratch."

" Don't believe him," said Richard. " He wants a doctor to patch it up properly. He can now tell you, at first hand, what it feels like to get a flesh wound from an automatic."

" Let's get inside," said Fane.

" Where's Mother? " Richard asked the question as Fane took Martin's sound arm lightly, and led the way towards the front of the house.

No one else was in the square hall. A large painting, a woodland scene, was opposite the door, and the light over it was on; on either side was a shot-gun. Two or three oak antiques stood about the polished floor. There was a chandelier, but that light wasn't on. The hall had a friendly, pleasing atmosphere. One door leading from it stood open; that led to the kitchen quarters.

"Upstairs with your young friend," said Fane dryly.

"Which one?" asked Richard.

"Never mind footling questions, telephone for Dr. Tucker," said Fane, and motioned to the telephone, which was by the side of the wide staircase. "Come upstairs and let me have a look at that arm, Martin."

The nickname "Scoop" was seldom used at home; it was kept for moments of real emotion.

"It's all right." Richard was already at the telephone. "Have you a Miss Barbara Marrison here?"

"Yes."

"Don't trust her!"

Fane smiled broadly.

"Very well," he said dryly. "Whether she can be trusted or not, she's going to wait until I've had a look at your arm. Have you told the police what happened?"

"Not yet."

"When you've finished with the doctor, call the Dorchester police," said Fane. "Ask for Inspector Medley, and if he's not there, Superintendent Burns."

He spoke in a calm voice, as he led the way upstairs, refusing to let Martin stay down until he'd looked at the wound. In figure and features he was more like Martin than Richard, but he wasn't so tall. He was plump without being really fat, wore a pale-blue shirt, with plenty of room at the collar, and a spotted white-and-blue tie. The coat fitted him well. His hair was iron grey, rather long, and growing well back from his forehead. As he went up the stairs, his limp was more noticeable than when he walked on level ground.

"What happened?" he asked, as they turned into the large bathroom on the first floor.

The lights came on as he pressed the switch, and shone on the white tiles and chromium; everything here was as modern as could be.

"We were held up on the road by three or four men."

"Three *or* four?"

Martin grinned, in spite of himself.

"Four! One of them gave me a hearty kick in the midriff, that's why I'm slow-moving."

"Oh. Sorry. We'd have done this downstairs if I'd known," said Fane. He pushed forward the bathroom stool, and Martin didn't protest about sitting down; he was glad to sit. His father took off his coat, smiled faintly at sight of the tourniquet, unfastened it, and held the arm out straight, using very little pressure. There was only slight pain, and the bleeding had almost stopped. He damped a sponge and washed the dried blood off, then peered at the wound. "I wouldn't call it a scratch, but it could be a lot worse," he said. "It won't give you a lot of trouble. Did you recognise these people?"

"One of them."

"Friend of yours?" asked Fane dryly.

"Not exactly. Look here, this Miss Marrison——"

"She's downstairs with the man who brought her, and she won't run away," said Fane. "Don't worry about them, old chap." He heard Richard running up the stairs, and glanced round at the door. "Was Tucker in?"

"He's coming right away."

"Good. Police?"

"Medley was there. I told him everything—that is, everything that happened on the road, and he's promised to do all that's necessary. He'll come round when he's finished, too. And to think we thought we could get away without telling the police about this!"

"You read too many books," said Fane, with a twinkle in his grey eyes. "Now, tell me what's happened to-day."

"Barbara Marrison is——" began Richard.

"I can tell you're both desperately anxious to see Barbara Marrison again, but she's quite prepared to wait," said Fane, "and if necessary she can wait for an hour or two. We may as well be comfortable, though. Have you had dinner?"

He led the way out of the bathroom.

"Oh, yes."

"Whisky, Martin?"

"I don't think so, I've had a spot," said Martin.

Fane opened the door of his study. It was a small, book-lined room, with a huge flat-topped desk, a type-writer sitting under a black cover, a few reference books on the desk and on a small table beside it. The walls were panelled half-way up, and above this, hanging on the cream background, were coloured pictures, well drawn, but none of them remarkable as works of art; all were water-colours, and on most was the name: *Jonathan Fane*. These were the original drawings of some of the picture jackets for his books. In one wide book-case, standing against a wall and leaving little room for anything else, were several hundred books, all in their jackets; and an astounding number bore the name of Jonathan Fane. It was familiar to the younger men, but they glanced round, and Martin smiled, Richard grinned puckishly. There were four comfortable arm-chairs, and little room for much else.

"Sit down," said Fane, and studied Martin intently. "You've stood up to it well, anyhow. Has this young rip been making a nuisance of himself?"

"You'd give him full marks," said Martin.

"Thanks," murmured Richard. "I'll do the same for you one of these days. I don't know whether it's *anno domini* or just the passing of time, but I thought the Master of Mystery wanted to hear our pulsating story."

And when he's heard it, he'll snatch the cover off that fiction machine there, and—sorry." He raised a hand, to acknowledge his father's pointed stare. "Blame it on excitement. Shall I talk?"

"I don't mind who tells it."

Martin nodded.

"Well, you won't believe it," said Richard, "but we'll both sign on the dotted line, if necessary. Mind you, I haven't actually seen the diamonds. I've only Martin's word about them. He's usually truthful. I—yes, I'm telling you!"

He told the story breezily and didn't spare the slang; that helped to make it vivid. Martin, leaning back with his head on a cushion, was surprised at the thoroughness of the detail and the smooth order of the narrative. There was practically nothing he had to add, except what had happened when he had been on his own.

"And that's my end," said Richard. "Now if I were to be offered a drink——"

"You know where it is," said Fane and waved a hand. "Don't overdo——"

He stopped speaking for a split second, then went on without a change of tone, but he looked meaningly towards the door and began to get up, waving a hand to the others to keep silent.

"—— it, to-night, Skip. That is, not until after you've seen Miss Marrison and her friend."

Richard, already standing up, moved swiftly towards the door, a questioning, hopeful look in his eyes. Fane nodded. Richard gripped the handle, turned it silently, and pulled the door open vigorously. The lighted landing was empty. He stepped outside, and saw no one; there were no doorways in which anyone could hide, no sound to suggest that anyone else was upstairs. He came back, smiling, and brushing his hair back from his forehead.

"Your mistake. You ought to stick to the typewriter, Pop."

" I'll pop you," said Fane, and chuckled. " You were quick off the mark, I'll say that for you. There's hope for you yet."

" Do you mean to say you did that to see how I'd react? " Richard howled.

" I did."

" The man isn't to be trusted," said Richard disgustedly. " I'll catch you on the bend for that, honoured sir. Seriously, what does Barbara——"

The telephone bell rang, and Fane answered at once, looked surprised, and said:

" For you, Martin."

Martin took the receiver.

" Hallo? "

" Tom here," said Rowbottom promptly. " No sign of Pete at the cottage, but I've fixed it with a fisherman who has a cottage nearby to telephone if he should turn up. I'm doing all I can this end."

" Oh—fine."

" 'Bye," said Tom.

Martin rang off, and explained.

" Now let me hear your part," said Fane when Martin had finished.

" You're not human," groaned Richard. " By the time we see the girl, Tucker will be here. That'll be another delay. Then Mother will come down, and by the time she's got over the fond greeting and been convinced that Martin ought not to be in an isolation ward, we'll find that Barbara's gone home. She said she couldn't possibly be away from London to-night, didn't she? "

Martin, feeling much better, shrugged and smiled and told his story briefly. He didn't elaborate and didn't use slang; that made it rather less vivid than Richard's, although some parts had more meat. He went into some detail about Pete Dunn—his almost reluctant affection for his brother, and the probability that he'd known for some time that Raymond was going to the bad.

108

Fane leaned back, pulling at his pipe in much the same way that Martin often did, and when it was over he sat smoking, as if there were all the time in the world.

"You say Pete's overworking," said Fane.

"Crazily. He's either at the office or stuck down in his cottage, working like stink. Tom and I were talking about it a few days ago. In fact, one of the reasons for planning the holiday was to get Pete away."

"Never mind me," said Richard. "Now, enough of that! It's time we saw Barbara."

Fane took his pipe from his lips.

"Miss Barbara Marrison tells me that she is an insurance company's special investigator. Her company, the Relvon, insured the Rossmore diamonds, paid out thirty-five thousand pounds after their loss, and has been trying to trace them ever since. She has brought with her another private detective, a Mr. Robertson, of the Robertson Agency, which has been commissioned to help her. Other jewels besides the Rossmore diamonds might be involved." Fane was smiling urbanely as he stood up. "Of course, they may be lying, but I shouldn't think so. Coming to find out? We won't tell them where you've put the diamonds, of course, until we've made sure they're honest."

. . . . .

Barbara had taken off her coat. She wore a lemon-coloured blouse, and if there had been any doubts about the shapeliness of her figure, they vanished now. Her hair looked perfectly groomed—dark hair, with a natural wave. Her complexion was perfect, and her eyes were clear—and mildly amused. As she stood up, Martin watched her; and felt as he had done twice before. He also felt a great relief.

Barbara's companion was a middle-aged man, with grey hair and a greying brown moustache, wearing a brown suit. He was on the portly side, and smaller than Fane. He smiled faintly, and had a curiously superior manner.

" Hallo, Bar," said Richard brightly.

" Hallo, Richard. Martin, is your arm——"

" Nothing," said Martin; and glowed, for that was the first time she had used his Christian name. He saw his father smile, and didn't care if he grinned his head off. He went and took the girl's hand. " Why in blazes didn't you tell us? "

She laughed, not too freely.

" She suspected you of complicity in the theft of the Rossmore diamonds," said Fane mildly.

" *What?* " Richard gasped.

" I didn't exactly suspect——" Barbara began hastily.

" Shall we say that she didn't feel she could tell you everything until she'd consulted me? " asked Robertson promptly. " I was in Guildford. As soon as she told me what had happened, I decided that the best thing was to come down here and tell you the whole story, in the hope that you could help. There were certain indications that you might be involved—by accident, of course," he added hastily. " No one in his senses would suspect the sons of Jonathan Fane——"

" When you know my sons, you'll suspect them of anything," Fane said, his eyes twinkling. " Certainly you can give them credit for thinking that they might make good amateur detectives. They probably think it's in their blood."

" Barbara," said Richard solemnly, " I shall not forgive you."

" I'm sorry, but——" Barbara began.

She didn't have to finish, for a bell rang faintly, and made them all glance round. At the same moment the door opened and Mrs. Jonathan Fane came hurrying in. Her eyes lit up at the sight of Richard and Martin, then her gaze fell to Martin's arm, and she caught her breath.

"It's nothing to worry about, Mother," Martin said quickly. "Tucker's going to have a look at it, and he's on his way."

Evelyn Fane took off the lightly wound handkerchief very gently, had one quick look, paled, and said:

"Don't be ridiculous. You ought to be in bed."

"Now don't fuss."

"What on earth have you been doing?" his mother demanded, and her grey-green eyes sparkled. "You send an hysterical girl here for me to look after, getting round your father without saying a word to me. Then people come in the middle of the night and say you're mixed up with some diamond thieves, or something. Then——"

The door opened, and a black face appeared at the door; a smiling face, with gleaming white teeth and grizzled hair. Obviously Barbara and the man had seen the Negro before, for they showed no surprise.

"Doctor Tucker, he's come," announced the Negro, in a soft, soothing voice. "Shall I bring him in, sah?"

"Yes, Sampson," said Jonathan Fane.

"At least you had the good sense not to wait until morning," said his wife. "That's a wonder. Before we know where we are, we'll have the police here."

"They won't be likely to arrest you," said Fane mildly. "Martin's all right, darling, and everything will work out."

He crossed to his wife and took her arm; she shook his hand off.

Doctor Tucker came bustling in, a short, plump, bald-headed man, wearing a dinner-jacket and carrying a small pig-skin case. He looked surprised at the number of people there, nodded vaguely to everyone, and made a beeline for Mrs. Fane. He took one look at Martin's arm, and smiled; he had a boyish smile and a soothing voice.

" Pooh, what's all the fuss about? "

" Fuss! " exclaimed Mrs. Fane. " Can't you see——"

" Just a scratch," said Tucker, and winked at Martin. " We'll soon put that right. Better go to the bathroom."

" We'll use the downstairs cloakroom," Fane said, without saying why. " How is Gillian Dunn, darling? "

" Asleep at last, thank goodness."

" That's fine. Scoop could do with a good strong cup of tea," Fane said. " So could I! Have a word with Sampson, if you think you can trust him to make tea. It's almost the only thing he can't make."

Fane went out with Tucker and Martin, leaving his wife frowning towards the door. Richard moved across to her, and slid an arm round her waist.

" You're looking wonderful," he said. " Teach me the secret of eternal youth, will you? "

She glared at him; and the glare changed to a smile, she put up a hand and tweaked his left ear, which stuck out slightly more than the right.

" You needn't think you can blarney me."

" I wouldn't dream of it! Shall I go and make that tea, or——"

" I'll do it," she said, and bent a look upon Barbara and Robertson, which had no great friendliness in it. " You look after our *guests*." She swept towards the door, and Richard smothered a grin, and couldn't hide the affection in his eyes. She turned round from the door, and added emphatically, " When I come back, I shall want to know everything."

" Oh, you shall! "

Richard was like her, in looks and figure. She was tall and moved well, and her grey hair could not hide the youthfulness of her eyes. She was thin, perhaps a little too thin, and dressed in a maroon red linen suit, trimmed with white. It suited her perfectly. Her green-grey eyes were bright, would flash into anger quickly and as quickly break into a smile. Her lips were full, and she had large white teeth, beautifully kept.

She closed the door with a slam.

" My mother," said Richard to Barbara. " Of course, you've met. I don't think she approves of these goings-on, and I can't say I blame her. If you take my tip, you won't antagonise her any more than you have to. Repeat the suggestion that Martin and I may be crooks, and nothing Father can do will stop her from turning you out. Incidentally, why aren't you in London for the night, Bar? "

She laughed uneasily.

" I didn't think we'd be coming here. I had to go and see Mr. Robertson, and——"

" I think I know the rest," said Richard. " Let me tell you something else about the Fane family. Believe it or not, I am the only one who's absolutely normal." His eyes gleamed. " As you can see! The great Jonathan Fane has a second mission, besides writing whodunits—he is always putting the world right. He has a pretty wide general knowledge and a habit of thinking he can do everyone's job a little better than they can themselves. You'd be surprised how often he's right, too! And as for Martin—that's what I really started to say. Martin is ten years older than his age. He has strong convictions and a peculiar and almost fanatical devotion to the truth. Consequently, an aversion to lies. If you want to get on well with Martin, Bar, tell the simple truth or don't say anything at all. He can forgive evasions, but not the downright lie. What on earth made you think we were mixed up in this business? "

" Hadn't we better wait until everyone's here to-gether? " asked Robertson, hastily.

He looked a little troubled, as if he were beginning to realise that Richard was partly right; if he had expected

a normal family, he was going to be grievously disappointed.

"I suppose so," said Richard. "Drink, anyone?
In five minutes we're all going to be offered tea. The
Master is a teetotaller, and whether in the Arctic Circle
or the tropics, he likes his tea first thing in the morning
and last thing at night."

"If there could be a whisky-and-soda," Robertson said
hopefully.

He looked a self-important man who disliked the need
for asking favours.

"Of course. Bar?"

"I'll have tea."

"Worming yourself into the parents' good graces,"
accused Richard.

He went to a cocktail cabinet, poured out a whisky-
and-soda for Robertson and a gin-and-French for himself, sipped it, watching Barbara all the time with a smiling
gaze, and then turned as the door opened.

Sampson put his head round the door, and radiated
goodwill.

"Massa Richard, can yo' spare one minute, sah?"

"I knew I'd have to make the tea," said Richard
resignedly. "Mother's now telling Doc Tucker how to
treat a gunshot wound, and Father's correcting her.
More about that later."

He put down his glass and went out, leaving Barbara
and Robertson looking at each other in some alarm. He
closed the door.

"What is it, Sampson?"

"Yo' father would like to see yo' in the cloakroom,
sah."

"More conspiracy, is it? How are you?"

"I'm fine, sah, just fine."

"I'll be seeing you in the morning," said Richard.
"We'll go rabbit-shooting."

He squeezed the Negro's arm, and went towards the
cloakroom which was on the other side of the hall, but

stopped before he reached the door. His mother called out from the stairs, and came hurrying down. She held a small jewel-case in her hand. He waited for her.

"Seriously, you're looking great," he said.

"Am I, darling? It's nice of you to say so." Evelyn Fane wasn't thinking about that. "You haven't been doing anything really silly, have you? I mean, that girl upstairs. She *looks* lovely, but if I were you——"

"No romance," said Richard firmly.

Evelyn's gaze was very direct.

"Promise?"

"Neither Martin nor I have become enamoured of Gillian Dunn," said Richard. "I'm not so sure about Barbara Marrison, Martin's been looking at her with a strange glow in his eyes. I haven't noticed him quite like that before. I can't say I dislike the wench myself." He squeezed his mother's waist, and touched the case. "What's that?"

"Your father wants them," said Evelyn Fane, and led the way to the cloakroom.

Tucker had examined Martin's stomach, pronounced it only severe bruising as far as he could judge, and had finished with the wound, and was tying a bandage round Martin's powerful forearm. Martin's colour was much better. There was a strong smell of antiseptic, and Tucker's case lay open on a chair. He started to put his instruments and oddments away. Jonathan Fane was sitting on the lavatory pan.

"Come and sit here, Evelyn," he said, getting up slowly, and held out his hand for the case. "Both of them in here?"

He opened the case. Two rings were inside, fitted into little slots against a background of black velvet. They were diamonds; nothing like the size of those which Martin had handled that morning, but nevertheless, big stones. Richard eyed them thoughtfully, and Martin, thinking of the wash-leather bag and not knowing why his father had sent for these, put an empty pipe to his lips.

"You won't want me any longer," said Tucker. "If the girl upstairs is asleep she'll probably rest until to-morrow midday. She was suffering from exhaustion as much as anything else."

He closed his case.

"Stay a minute," said Fane. "That's if you've time."

"Well——" Tucker put his case down.

"Have a look at these, Martin," said Fane, and held the two rings out. "They're your mother's. How do the stones compare with those you saw this morning?"

Martin took the rings, held them on the palm of his hand, saw the shoots of light spring from the diamonds. He had seen the others in daylight, and there was only electric light here; but it seemed to make these stones brighter than the others.

"Well, they're smaller."

"The others must be whoppers! See any difference?"

"Only in size."

"I mean, between those two," said Fane.

Richard gave a low-pitched whistle, as if he had realised what his father was getting at. Martin looked puzzled, examined the jewels again, picked each up in turn and looked at it directly beneath the light. Tucker, looking more than ever like a large boy, stared from one man to the other, as if he couldn't understand what all this was about. Evelyn Fane sat watching; her gaze shifted quickly from her husband to her two sons.

Martin said, "No, I can't say I do. Why?"

"There was a time when I was poor," said Fane, smiling faintly. "You two reprobates have always had a silver spoon in your mouths, and probably don't believe me, but it's true. That "—he pointed—" was the first ring I ever bought your mother. It cost five pounds, and was dear at the price. That "—he pointed again—" was one I bought to replace it, later. The same size, as far as possible, and worth—well, never mind what it's worth. It's a real diamond, the other is good paste. Can you be sure that the ones you found were real diamonds, Martin, or could they have been paste? "

. . . . .

After a long, tense pause, in which Richard rocked to and fro on his heels and Dr. Tucker rubbed his fleshy chin softly, yet making a slight noise, Evelyn Fane jumped up.

" I must go and make that tea," she said, and hurried out.

The others hardly seemed to notice her departure.

Martin drew a deep breath.

" They could have been paste. I'm no judge. I took it for granted they were real."

" I'll lend you some books to read! We've another reason why we won't tell Robertson and the Marrison woman what happened this morning," went on Fane urbanely. " Not yet, at all events. I——"

He broke off, and glared at Richard. Richard had stopped swaying to and fro, and was laughing; it was gusty laughter, he tried to stifle it by clapping a hand over his mouth, but it shook his whole body, and an occasional splutter escaped. He couldn't stop. He backed to the wall and leaned against it heavily, still laughing. Fane's annoyance faded, Martin's lips began to curve.

" I think I'd better give *him* a sedative," Tucker said brightly. " He'll get hysterical next. Why did you ask me to stay, Fane? "

" I wanted someone outside the family to hear Martin say that." Fane picked up the doctor's case. " I'll see you to the door, Tuck. Try and stop him, Scoop," he added to Martin, and left the two brothers together.

Richard drew his hand away and laughed explosively; and Martin's grin widened. Richard pressed his hands against his forehead, began to laugh more moderately, went across to the hand-basin, and rinsed his face in cold water. That seemed to steady him effectively. He turned round, dabbing at his face with a yellow towel.

" Sorry, old chap. I couldn't help it. You, chasing to the bank thinking you had a fortune. The gents on the road, getting wounded and taking that kind of chance, and possibly for paste. It's gorgeous. I couldn't tell t'other from which, either, paste or the real stuff is all the same to me. But—not for the Maestro. You know, he *knows* a thing or two, and doesn't miss much in the way of possibilities."

Martin nodded soberly.

Fane came back.

" The tea's just gone in, we'd better hurry," he said. " But before we go—don't forget this. Whether the diamonds you found were real or fakes, Martin, the important thing is to find Raymond Dunn and Pete. I don't like to think that Pete's in serious trouble. So be careful what you say to these self-styled detectives."

15

EVELYN FANE dispensed tea and biscuits with as much care as she would have used at a tea-party of social importance; only Robertson refused a cup, and that self-consciously. They sat round the large, high-ceilinged room in comfortable Knoll-type arm-chairs. The *décor* was delightful—maroon red and dark blue against cream walls. All the pictures were portraits; all were good. Most of the furniture was antique, helping to make it a restful yet striking room.

"As far as I can make out, from both sides of the story," said Jonathan Fane, leaning back in an easy-chair with his legs stretched straight out, as if the only thing that really mattered was physical comfort, "the immediate problem turns on why you are so anxious to see Pete Dunn, Miss Marrison."

"I've tried to tell you," she said.

"You haven't tried to tell us," remarked Richard.

"I know. It wasn't easy, you see. We've suspected a gang of jewel thieves for some time, and know quite a lot about them. One of the significant things is that a great deal of stolen jewellery is sold, a long time after the thefts, without being altered at all. Usually stones are cut down so that it's impossible to recognise or identify them, and when that happens there's little hope of finding them. But if we're right about this gang, they keep the jewels whole—and when it is safe to sell, they get a much bigger price for them."

Robertson nodded, portentously.

"So we're always on the look-out. The Rossmore Diamonds are nearly perfect stones, and would fetch a lot more in their original form than if they were cut.

A few weeks ago we heard that one of them had been
offered for sale, in London. It——"

"Where did you hear that from?" asked Jonathan Fane.
"Well——"

"We hear a lot of rumours," said Robertson sonorously.
"It isn't always possible to reveal the source of the information, Mr. Fane. *We* learn a lot that the police
never know, because our interest is getting the jewels
back, not sending the thieves to jail."

Martin put his head on one side, and looked as if he
either disliked Mr. Robertson or else disapproved of
something he had said. His father nodded.

"We traced the seller, a man named Dunn—Raymond
Dunn," Barbara went on hurriedly. "So we went
closely into his history. He's a young man, as you know.
He inherited a small fortune from a grandparent, ran
through it in a few months, lived wildly and extravagantly,
betting, wine—the usual things. Then he got married,
bought a small house, and seemed to settle down. For a
few months, we gathered, he lived a fairly normal sub-
urban life, attending to his own affairs, dabbling in the
Stock Exchange, buying and selling small businesses. That
period ended twelve months ago. As far as we have been
able to find out, from that time on he began to go down-
hill. He lost heavily on the dogs and at race-meetings,
began to mortgage his property, and lost his self-control
completely." Barbara talked now as if she were reading
from a report. "He was known to have a lot of acquaint-
ances among the worst types at the dog tracks and among
the racing fraternity. He began to worry less and less
about the kind of deal he put through—and twice, we
know, handled stolen goods. Then he offered one of the
Rossmore stones for sale, to a man who is usually in the
market. But the man was being watched closely by the
police, and wouldn't buy."

"Who is the man?" asked Jonathan Fane.

Robertson said quickly, "We can't go into details like
that at this stage."

" I see," said Fane, and made the word sound ominous.
" Go on, Miss Marrison."

Barbara sipped her tea, Evelyn Fane looked to see if
there were any empty cups.

" We watched Raymond Dunn very closely, and—and I
met his brother."

" Did you tell him who you were? " asked Fane.

Barbara hesitated—and then forced a smile.

" Of course I didn't. I managed to get an introduction,
and we became friendly. After a while, I felt quite sure
that he wasn't involved in any of this. I discovered that
he was always being worried for loans by his brother,
and wasn't sure that Raymond was honest. So the day
before yesterday—after consulting Mr. Robertson I told
him what I was doing. He was rather shaken, of course,
but we didn't quarrel. He promised to do everything
he could to find out if Raymond had these diamonds, or
whether he was acting for someone else."

" Did you know Raymond was missing? " asked Fane.

" I knew he hadn't been home for several days. But
that wasn't unusual."

Barbara paused and stretched out her hand for another
cup of tea, which Evelyn Fane gave her without a word.
Evelyn went back and sat on a pouf, with her legs
stretched out in front of her, and spent most of her time
looking from Barbara to Martin. Martin did not remove
his gaze from the girl's face.

" Pete hoped to have some more information for me by
last night. Then he telephoned about not being able to
get away, and meeting me at Guildford. He'd often
mentioned you, I knew about the coming tour. When he
said he'd meet me under the clock, I thought that he'd
settled everything to his own satisfaction and was ready
to go off on holiday. I was disappointed. Because if it
meant serious trouble for his brother, I didn't think he
would leave. He's always seemed fond of Raymond,
although he was exasperated with the way he went
on."

" People did get fond of Raymond," Richard remarked.
" Gillian, for instance."

" Everyone was attracted by him, and he was his
family's darling," Martin said. " His grandfather left
him a small fortune, and only a trifle to Pete. Raymond
was pampered and spoiled. That's partly responsible for
this. It often exasperated Pete, but——"

He shrugged his shoulders.

" That doesn't help to answer the question—what's
happened to Pete? "

Richard dug his hands deep in his pocket as he spoke.

Barbara said slowly, " There was one other possibility,
of course—that when he wanted me to meet him at Guildford, he was going to tell me *you* knew something about it.
I couldn't ignore that."

" It never does to let the heart rule the head, in *our*
profession," said Robertson heavily.

For the first time Evelyn Fane bent a glance of approval
at him.

" What shook you when I made that remark about him
being at death's door or he would have turned up? "
asked Richard, lightly.

Barbara hesitated, and looked at Robertson; she consulted him too often, in Martin's opinion; she had a
much better mind. But if he were the boss——

Robertson squared his shoulders, as if aware that he was
going to make a pronouncement of great importance. He
looked round at everyone in turn, obviously to make sure
that he held their attention. Evelyn Fane got up,
abruptly, and collected plates; a measure of her opinion
of Robertson. He waited until she had settled down, and
looked at her disapprovingly. The others gave him all
the attention he could hope to get.

" I am glad you asked that, Mr. Fane. You must be
told that if we are right about the identity of some of the
people concerned in these crimes, they are desperadoes.
You will have gathered that from the incident on the road.
There was, therefore, always a measure of danger for

anyone who was investigating it. I may say that was one of the reasons why I was reluctant to work with a young lady, but Miss Marrison had great courage—*great* courage—and unusual ability, and of course, I had my instructions from the Insurance Company. The circumstances warranted the risk. She was aware, then, of the possibility of danger, and the remark which you made flippantly had a sinister meaning for her."

No one spoke for a moment.

Barbara said, "I couldn't imagine why Pete hadn't turned up, unless he was in difficulty. You two were there, and he wasn't. There was obviously the possibility that if you were involved, you knew where he was. Call me ridiculous, if you like, but——"

"*I* should say you took leave of your senses," remarked Evelyn Fane bluntly; but a smile softened the words. "Jonathan, it's after midnight. Martin's looking tired out, and I don't care what the doctor says, he ought to rest after losing all that blood. You will have to sleep in the old playroom, Miss Marrison. Richard will show you to your room, Mr. Robertson."

She stood up.

"You're very kind," Robertson began, "but——"

"Oh, we can't possibly impose on you." Barbara sprang to her feet. "We'll find a hotel in Dorchester, or——"

"They closed an hour ago," said Richard. "You'll have to impose. Bad luck!" He smiled broadly at her, and yawned. "I'm getting a bit tired myself."

"Before the party breaks up," said Martin heavily, "we've one or two other things to mention. Have either of you any idea where Pete is now?"

"Obviously not," said Robertson.

"Or where Raymond is?"

"We are completely mystified."

"Did Gillian say anything?" Martin asked his mother. Evelyn laughed.

"She talked a lot of nonsense about never seeing him

again, but she hasn't said anything at all helpful. Don't worry about it any more to-night, go to bed. *I'm* tired out. Jonathan——"

" You go up," said Jonathan Fane. " I won't be long."

" Don't keep the boys up, *please*."

" Oh, they can go to bed," said Fane carelessly. He stood up. " What made you so sure these people would be violent, Mr. Robertson? You know they are now, did you know before? "

" Several burglaries in a series have been committed with violence," said Robertson. " If we suspect the right people, they're really dangerous. They're led by a man named Rummy, called Smart Rummy, whom no one seems to have seen. He's the mystery man behind the whole thing."

" Jonathan! " exclaimed Evelyn Fane, sharply.

" Yes, darling? "

" You must go round the house yourself and make sure all the doors are locked. We ought to have the shutters fastened, too. Richard, you can help. I——"

The door opened, slowly, and she happened to catch sight of it and started violently. Fane moved swiftly to her side; her start and the stealthy opening of the door had made the men stiffen, Martin felt his heart thumping —until a grizzled head appeared at the door and Sampson gave a timid smile as he came farther into the room.

" Massa Fane, there's a gennulman asking fo' you, a Massa Medley. Shall I tell him to come in? "

" Medley! " exclaimed Evelyn. " *Inspector* Medley? "

" He's quite safe, he's only a policeman," said Fane. " If he thinks it's necessary, we'll have some police on guard in the grounds, my sweet. You needn't worry. Care to see the Inspector? " he asked Robertson.

" Of course."

" *I'm* going to bed," said Evelyn.

Richard went up with her, probably so that he could see the detective. Medley was a big, dark, stolid man, who seemed to move as if it were an effort. Evelyn said she was terribly sorry he'd been called out so late, she did hope he'd forgive them; and Richard poked her gently in the ribs as they went upstairs.

Fane went into the hall, and told Medley quickly about the diamonds in the bank. The rest, he said, could be told with everyone present.

Richard was down again by the time Medley had been introduced to the others in the drawing-room. He listened with rapt attention, made a few notes but no comment until it was over. Then he spoke in a deep, formal voice.

Since Richard had telephoned, the motor cycle had been collected and was being examined, they would probably be able to trace it. Signs of the shooting had been discovered at the dangerous corner, and in view of what had happened he had placed four men in the grounds. It would probably be wise to let them stay all night.

It was one o'clock before Medley left, with Martin's bank receipt for the diamonds in his pocket, and twenty minutes past before Martin got into bed.

The last half-hour had left him confused, he was more tired than he had realised, and the kick in the stomach was still painful. The man who had kicked him was probably Smart Rummy. Smart Rummy didn't seem to belong to real life, but might have been a creation of his father's fertile brain. It would be easy to go to sleep and wake up thinking that he had been reading one of the latest books and dreaming about it. He smiled wryly to himself as he moved his left arm cautiously and wondered how long it would be before he had full use of it. He dozed off.

Now and again he smiled, because he knew the truth about Barbara Marrison. He had no doubt that it was the truth. Robertson wouldn't have been so happy at meeting Medley if there were any serious holes in his story. It was a queer job for a girl to have; but it seemed to pay well. He wouldn't have thought—— He dozed off.

It was dark when he woke—pitch dark. He had no idea what time it was, but heard the bedside clock ticking. His room was a small one, opposite Richard's, and on a half-landing; there was a bathroom handy, but no other bedrooms. The ticking of the clock seemed very loud. The events of the previous day began to crowd his mind; obviously they were working on him subconsciously, he was probably going to have a restless night. He was comfortable and warm, anyhow, and there was no pain worth calling pain, only a slight ache in his stomach; that had been some kick.

He heard a sound; something small had fallen on the dressing-table.

Next moment he heard a faint gasp.

16

MARTIN's heart thumped wildly, but he didn't move. No
other sound followed that gasp, which had been little
more than a catch of breath. He even closed his eyes.
After a long pause, he opened them again. Had he
imagined it? If anyone were in the room, could they
be as quiet as they were now? He looked towards the
windows. Clouds obscured the stars, and there was no
light, just a faint greyness; he could make out the shape
of the dressing-table mirror against the window. The
sound had come from there; he felt quite sure of it. On
either side there was opaque darkness; anyone could
hide there.

If he moved he would give away the fact that he was
awake. He was very conscious of his useless left arm; of
the fact that these rooms were so far apart from the rest
of the house. Richard might be awake; but was that
likely after the tiring day?

His agitation settled, and he was beginning to tell himself that it had been imagination, when he heard a faint
rustle of movement. Then a figure appeared against the
greyness of the window; he couldn't be sure whether it
was a man or woman. He thought he saw a pale blur of
white, about face level; then he closed his eyes.

He heard a faint click, and was aware of light. He
peered through his lashes. Someone was shining a torch
towards him. It wasn't a shaft of light, but a diffused
glow spreading over a wide radius, with a patch of yellow
at the centre. The sound of movement was repeated,
and the light drew nearer. Gradually its character
altered: the glow faded, but a single beam shone out and

fell upon his face. It rested there only for a moment, and moved on.

The marauder had a torch, and by twisting the head could spread a glow or else give a concentrated beam of light. Whoever it was, was trying to make sure that Martin was still asleep. His eyelids twitched a little, but he didn't think they had while he had been spotlighted.

He ventured to look through his lashes again.

The light was now diffused and turned away from him towards the dressing-table. A hand was stretched out, moving different things—the little piles of copper and silver, his keys, his watch, his wallet; he always emptied his pockets before going to bed. Nothing was taken away. The vague figure turned towards the chair over which his clothes were folded; Richard had come in to fold them for him. The light shone upon the clothes; the marauder was going through the pockets.

He eased himself up in bed, making no sound that the other noticed. He turned towards his right side, so that he could spring out more easily; but for the injured left arm, it would be simple to make a capture.

The marauder finished with the clothes, turned, and passed the mirror; by a trick of light and the direction in which the torch was turned for a moment, he recognised the reflection in the glass.

His visitor was Barbara Marrison.

.   .   .   .   .

She faded into the darkness, and only the light shone out in front of her. It seemed to get lower, and he saw it shining on his suit-case—he had brought only one, the hand-trunk was in Richard's room. She went down on her knees, and he could hear the faint sound as she tried to open it; that was easy, he had unlocked it to get his pyjamas out, but hadn't unpacked.

She pulled up the lid.

He could see the light and her hands, as she probed in the corners, took out several oddments and put them aside. She took out some folded clothes, too, and appeared to take great care not to unfold them. At last she seemed satisfied; and as far as he could judge, she put everything back and shut the case.

After the click as the lock fastened, the light went out; and the darkness seemed more intense than ever.

He heard the rustle of sound as she stood up.

Had she finished?

She was looking for the diamonds, of course; she wasn't satisfied about them. It was easy to believe that, because he wanted to reject the obvious explanation: that she was simply a thief. She had convinced him, but he hadn't liked Robertson; nor had his mother, whose quick judgment of character was very shrewd.

No, Barbara hadn't done; she went to the wardrobe. There was nothing else in the room where she could search, except the bedside table. Obviously she had searched the dressing-table before he had wakened.

She finished with the wardrobe; that didn't take long, because it was practically empty and there were no drawers in it. Yet everything seemed to have taken an age; he had reached a stage where he couldn't keep still; his nerves kept twitching. Her stealthy movements, that thoroughness with which she worked, had an uncanny effect; it was like watching a ghost.

The light shone towards him again, flickered over his face, and then stayed somewhere near. He opened his eyes a fraction; the beam shone on the bedside table and the clock. He felt himself go rigid, as he thought she moved towards the bed, and closed his eyes just in time, for the light shone strongly into his face.

She seemed satisfied. She drew nearer.

When he opened his eyes again, the merest fraction, she was standing by the bedside and pulling gently at the one drawer in the table. That was with her right hand; in her left she held the torch. Suddenly she moved it towards him, but didn't seem to know that he was awake; the beam shone inside the drawer.

He shot out his right arm, gripped her wrist and jerked

himself upright. She gasped and dropped the torch, and it went out. He moved his left arm, found the hanging light switch which was just above his head, and pressed. Light flooded over the bed and the girl, as she struggled but couldn't free herself from his grip.

The grip was very hard; and painful.

" I shouldn't try any more," he said. " You'll only hurt yourself."

She stopped struggling. She wore a man's raincoat over a pair of pyjamas that his mother had lent her. Her eyes were rounded in mingled distress and dismay. Her hair was rumpled, she had on no make-up. She just stood rigid, staring at him. He pushed back the bed-clothes, and swung his legs off the bed, still holding her. He stood up, let her go, and stepped swiftly to the door. He turned the key in the lock, and took the key out.

She didn't move.

" Now what's all this about? " he demanded.

She didn't answer; he didn't think she could find her voice. Quite suddenly her legs seemed to crumple beneath her, and she dropped on to the bed. She put a hand to her head, but didn't speak.

" I feel desperately sorry for you," Martin said sardonically. " Getting caught must have a nasty effect on burglars. What's it all about? "

She licked her lips as she looked up at him.

" I thought—you'd sleep like a log."

" That's what didn't happen," he said.

He turned round and took a lightweight dressing-gown from the foot of the bed, and slipped it on; it wasn't easy with his injured left arm, but he managed it, and pretended there was no stiffness. He dropped the door-key into a pocket. Then he sat on a chair in front of the wardrobe and watched her; and felt anger welling up inside him. Through that anger there came something else which he couldn't explain. She looked helpless and wan, and that wasn't surprising. Without make-up she had a quality it was hard to describe; some of the perfection was gone, but she was still lovely and whole-some to look at. If she were relaxed and not frightened, she would be——

He stifled the thought.

" Inspector Medley would gladly get out of bed to come and talk to you," he said harshly.

She nodded vaguely.

" Shake out of it! What do you want? "

She said slowly, " You know what I want."

He could guess, but wasn't prepared to make anything easy for her. He wanted to hurt her; not physically, but mentally. She was frightened, and he wanted to put greater fear into her. He knew that this was because she had hurt him; he did not reason that it was madness to feel any emotion for a girl he'd known for only a few hours.

" If you don't tell me why you came, *Miss* Marrison, I'll——"

" Oh, don't pretend," she said, more vigorously. " I want those diamonds."

" I see. Perhaps you'll tell me when I stole them, why I stole them, and——"

" I don't know whether you stole them in the first place. I know you have them now," she said.

" You're quite wrong."

" I'm not wrong. You took them from Raymond Dunn's house. It wasn't Garrett, he hadn't time, and he ran away. In any case, you wouldn't have been held up on the road if he'd taken them. So it must have been you. I know you took them, because I've seen the rifled deed-box. They were inside that. Why don't you stop lying? You'll only get yourself into trouble. You may think you're helping Pete or his brother, but you're not. You're inviting yourself to prison."

She made that sound almost convincing.

" How do you know they were in that deed-box? "

" Isn't that obvious? It's hard to believe you're a thief, but——"

" It isn't hard to believe you are," Martin said.

She didn't answer.

" Supposing you now tell me the truth instead of the cock-and-bull story you expected me to believe downstairs? "

" You know the truth," said Barbara, more steadily. " You know more than I do, you know where the diamonds are."

" If you'd found them here, what would you have done? Taken them off in the morning and handed them over to the insurance company? " He laughed; he didn't sound amused. " I don't think! You——"

" I should have done just that," she said, " and for some crazy reason I shouldn't have said where I'd found them. I'd have made something up. I don't want to get you into trouble with the police. That's why I came and looked myself. If we don't find them, we'll have to tell the police we know you have them." She had dropped easily into that " we ", as if Robertson knew what she was doing. " They'll have to search. You'll find it's more difficult to deal with them than to deal with me."

He didn't answer.

" Where *are* they? " she demanded, as if she thought he was weakening; she actually got up from the bed.

" Sit down! " he snapped.

She sat down hurriedly; and the springs creaked slightly.

" I'll tell you when you can move. So if you haven't found the diamonds to-night, the police will search in the morning."

" They'll have to be told." The girl sounded almost desperate, stood up again and, because he didn't snap at her, came towards him. He thought she might try to get away, but she didn't glance at the door, just stood in front of him with one hand outstretched, appealingly. " Martin, don't meddle in this ugly business. Don't try and be a character in one of your father's books. The police won't be interested in his reputation or in yours. And Smart Rummy certainly won't, that man is dangerous. You don't need any more telling, surely. Please—let me have the diamonds, and——"

She stopped, because his expression had changed. He began to smile, then to chuckle; it was a deep, whole-hearted sound, and bewildered her. She stepped back a pace, frowning down at him, backed away farther when he got up, put out his right hand, and gripped her arm.

He stopped chuckling, but still smiled.

" This is serious," she said weakly.

" Oh, desperately! I'm just beginning to believe that you really came to try and help Richard and me out of a scrape."

She didn't speak.

" And that you really think we have the baubles and might be interested in making a fortune out of them! " The chuckle burst out again. " You're making mistakes, Barbara. We're both honest. Quite as honest as Pete Dunn."

" Martin! Is the packet of diamonds here, or isn't it? "

" It is not."

She said helplessly, " I felt absolutely sure it was."

The light shone fully on her face, and again he saw the change which could come over her. This was different, but had much in common with what had happened before. She looked more homely; attainable? Her hair was untidy, and her cheeks and nose rather shiny. Her eyes began to shine. He realised then that the change, when it came, always began in her eyes; they glowed. The weight of anxiety and uncertainty lifted, and he sensed that for the first time she felt quite sure of him.

Suddenly his right arm slipped round her waist; as suddenly, they faced each other, their lips very close. His heart thumped, as it had when he had woken up. This was Richard's *forte*, not his. She yielded, very slightly—

133

and suddenly he pressed his lips against hers. When he drew back, her eyes were glistening, her lips were parted. He kissed her again, and her lips seemed to melt into his, he could feel the wild beating of her heart.

Then the door burst open.

BARBARA darted back as Martin's arm fell from her waist. He swung round towards the door with a flurry of alarm, as Barbara caught her breath.

Richard, in his pyjamas, hair tousled, hands raised, stared at them incredulously; gulped, opened his mouth as if to speak, gulped again, then let his hands flop to his sides. He took a step forward, then a step backwards, and stopped exactly where he had been when his first rush had come to a halt.

"What the devil are you doing?" growled Martin.

Richard closed his eyes.

"Dreaming," he said faintly.

He opened his eyes again, as Martin felt a flash of anger; he seldom felt really angry with Richard. Barbara stood quite still and silent.

"No, learning," Richard corrected. His voice was husky. "Don't fly off the handle, Scoop. I heard voices, thought you might be in trouble. Almost anything could happen to-night, couldn't it? My door-key fits yours, I was full of stealth and silence, and—I feel as if Mount Vesuvius is coughing up virgin snow."

"Idiot," growled Martin.

"My dear chap, I couldn't agree more. I will now beat a bewildered retreat. Er—the only thing I ought to mention, perhaps, is that if Mother's restless and starts worrying about you, she might drift along. I mean, she can stand most shocks, and if it were me she would simply raise her eyebrows and order Bar out of the house. Being you, she will feel as if the heavens have sent another deluge, she might even think that Bar's taking advantage

of you while you're in delirium, or something. Sorry
again. Good night."

" Come here, you oaf," said Martin.

" My dear chap——"

" You might like to know that Barbara burgled my
room," Martin said heavily.

" Oh. It didn't look like it. Depends what she came
to steal, of course. If I burble, I can't help it. I thought
I was a fast worker, but one look at Barbara, and I
decided that the first peck of a kiss was at least ten days
off."

" You addle-pated Don Juan, stop talking like a fool,"
growled Martin. " Shut the door and come and sit
down. Warm enough, Barbara? "

" Yes—thanks."

" Don't inquire about *my* health," said Richard.

" I'm not interested in your health. Barbara came and
looked through my room because she felt sure that I
had the diamonds. I've decided that she's everything
she says she is, and she's even beginning to believe in me."
Martin grinned, as if at the greatest joke in the world.
" And you."

" What I saw was the seal on the understanding," said
Richard. " In future I shall believe everything, even the
stories about pink elephants."

" What you saw has nothing to do with the problem.
Where is Pete, and where is Raymond Dunn? Barbara
really doesn't know where we might find them."

" Really," said Richard, politely. " I don't blame
her. Look, I must get back to bed. I've a considerable
shock to recover from, whether you believe it or not.
Don't ask me to wait outside and shout cave if anyone
happens to come and investigate the murmur of voices."
He backed to the door again. " Good night, Scoop.
'Night, Bar. Sleep happy."

He went out.

" He can't help being a fool," said Martin.

" We can't blame him for jumping to conclusions, ' said

136

Barbara. Her tone was light-hearted and the glow was back in her eyes. " I must go to my room. Good night."

He took her hand.

" You might regret a lot of things in the morning," Barbara said hurriedly, and freed herself. " No, I can go back alone—don't come with me—Scoop." She hesitated. " Why does he call you that, sometimes? "

" Old nickname, as a boy I was called Scoopy. I've never really known why. It doesn't matter, either."

" I rather like it."

" Barbara," began Martin, slowly but firmly.

Her eyes were radiant, as she interrupted him.

" Good night, Scoop," she said, and went out.

He didn't follow her to the door, but stood between it and the bed. He put his hand to his dressing-gown pocket, and felt the key. He smiled. He remembered Richard's expression when the door had burst open, and he grinned. He didn't feel tired, and nothing hurt. He felt that he wanted to celebrate. There was no whisper of doubt of Barbara in his mind. He went to the bed and looked down at it, let thoughts of what had happened since he had been disturbed run through his mind, punched the pillows and shook off his dressing-gown, then got into bed. He was stretching up for the light switch when the door opened, and Richard said:

" Alone, Lothario? "

Martin let his arm drop.

" Yes. Come in." Richard now wore a dressing-gown of pale blue. " I thought you were tired."

" That was only to give Barbara a broad hint," said Richard. A cigarette dangled from his lips, bobbing up and down as he talked. " How's the arm and tummy? "

" All right.'"

" Good. I just wanted you to know that I still don't believe it, and—ah—apologise for the intrusion."

" Ass."

" Thanks. And—ah—don't set too much store by anything, will you? " For Richard, he sounded em-

137

barrassed, and he looked wary. "Don't start screwing up your face like a gorilla, listen a moment. There's nothing you think about Barbara that I don't. We agree about her. On the other hand, she has done odd things. Never forget it. Everything she says may be on the level. If it proves not to be——"

"It is," Martin said abruptly.

Richard stole out of the room.

. . . . .

Richard was in the room again, next morning, with the sun shining in at the window and striking the side of his face. His smile wasn't his usual free and merry one. He was fully dressed, and had one hand in his pocket, a cigarette was burning in the other. By the side of the bed was a tea-tray, and he glanced at it, as Martin grunted, opened his eyes wider, and began to sit up. He forgot his injured arm, and winced. His stomach felt bruised.

"I'll lend a hand," said Richard hastily. He slid an arm round Martin's shoulders and helped; he had surprising strength. "Shall I pour out?"

"Thanks. What's the time?"

"About ten. Are you as bad as you look?"

"No."

Martin was thoughtful, couldn't understand the other's manner. Richard poured out easily, handed over a cup and saucer, and stood back.

"Lovely morning. Promise of a nice day. Gillian's still fast asleep. Mother's in a sunny mood, and is determined to keep us here for at least a week, it would be folly to take you round the country with only an arm and a half, wouldn't it? That kind of thing. The Maestro, believe it or not, is typing. Sampson knows a man who knows a man who has a Buick and is hoping to get a key for the luggage-boot."

Throughout all this, Martin sipped the hot tea.

"No news of Pete, of course. The police have gone, leaving a fellow on duty at the gate, a kind of token force.

No one appears to expect trouble by day, with the possible exception of Mother, who looks meaningly at every poker she passes. More tea?"

"In a minute," said Martin.

He didn't ask the question which had sprung to his mind minutes ago. Why hadn't Richard mentioned Barbara? Richard looked uneasy, drew at his cigarette, and turned to look out of the window. His back was very straight, his movements had a rippling ease. He swung round again.

"Barbara's gone. Went off during the night. The watching people were to stop people coming *in*. Robertson's with her, of course. I'm as sorry as hell."

.   .   .   .   .

He could telephone friends in Fleet Street and find out what was known, if anything, about the Robertson Agency and whether a Miss Barbara Marrison really worked for the Relvon Insurance Company; or he could harass the police until they found out. His father advised letting the police work at their own pace, but had nothing to say about calling Fleet Street.

Richard was moody; Barbara's defection, without leaving a word of explanation, seemed to affect him as much as it did Martin. Martin did not enjoy his breakfast.

Medley telephoned, just after twelve o'clock, to say that the wash-leather bag had been collected by the police and was being brought to Nairn Lodge; would Mr. Martin Fane please be in, in order to identify the diamonds? There was no news, said Medley, of the men who had staged the attack on the road. He was neither friendly nor particularly aloof, but very business-like.

Jonathan Fane's typewriter, going at furious speed, sounded clearly in the garden when Martin and Richard went out for a stroll. Evelyn had gone into the village, and would be back for lunch. An elderly gardener and a small boy were busy in the flower-garden, and on a normal morning Martin would have given himself time to relax and enjoy it. The colours had never been brighter;

there were masses of late wallflowers, the roses 'were
blooming, the lawns were trim and green from recent rains.

" How about cutting out the whole trip, and getting
back to the flat? " asked Richard abruptly. " It's not
fair to make anxiety for the parents. We could work,
too, which would take our minds off it, anyhow."

" Better stay," said Martin. " Mother would feel it
more if we were to leave."

He saw a movement at the end of the drive—a white-
clad figure with a black face. It was Sampson on a
bicycle, which he rode with furious energy, his feet almost
at right-angles to the pedals.

Sampson had come with the Fanes from the West
Indies; they had lived there for some years. He was in
the middle forties, had always wanted to live in England,
and appeared not only to revel in it but also determined
to show his gratitude at all times to Jonathan Fane. He
had been with the family for years; knew their foibles;
knew that each of them held him in real affection.

As he approached, he waved, nearly fell, recovered his
balance, and waved again. The front wheel turned
towards the bank. How he avoided crashing was a
minor miracle. His beam split his face in two, and he
didn't stop that furious pedalling. As he drew nearer,
they saw the sun glisten on something in his right hand.

" He's found a key," said Richard.

" Several, by the look of it."

Sampson drew up, jumped off the bicycle, let it fall
heavily, and jingled a dozen keys which were tied
together with a piece of string. He was sweating slightly,
and his breath came in little puffs.

" Morning, Massa Martin, sah! Glad to see yo'
looking so well again. How's yo' po' arm? "

" It's doing fine, thanks."

" Thank de good Lord for all His mussies," said Sampson. " How's dis, Massa Richard? " He jingled the
keys. " All dese are American cars, yes sah! I been
visiting garages all over Dorchester. One ob dem is

sho' to open dat boot ob yo' beautiful new car, I should say."

" If it doesn't, we can't say you haven't tried," said Richard. " Come and see if one fits."

" Sho' thing, Massa Richard, what yo' think I'se going to do? " Sampson clutched the keys firmly and led the way to the garage, chattering as he went in his husky, fascinating voice. He was unmoved by Martin's tension and Richard's moodiness; he had known that moodiness before and often wheedled Richard out of it. As he neared the garage, he rattled the keys more vigorously.

There was room for four cars; only two were in the garage, a Humber Snipe and Blond Beauty. Martin glanced at the spot where the Armstrong-Siddeley had been parked, and wondered if it had been put into the garage; he hadn't thought to ask.

" It sho' is de best ob Buicks I eber saw," declared Sampson, selecting a key and thrusting it into the lock of the luggage-hold. It wouldn't turn. His grin broadened, if that were possible, and he tried another with the same result. He began to chuckle, as he tried the third, fourth, and fifth, without result. The greater his fear of failure the louder he laughed.

Martin was seeing a girl's face, instead of the black man's.

Sampson pushed in the sixth key, and turned—and it moved easily. He snatched his hands away, clasped them above his head, and breathed:

" The Lord be praised, it's the right key. Hallelujah! " He grabbed the handle and pulled; he had to give the door a jerk, and staggered back as it opened. He peered inside, and started to say, " It must be de biggest——"

His voice trailed off. An expression of horror froze on his face.

Richard exclaimed; Martin felt his heart give a wild thump, then felt himself grow cold.

The body of a man was jammed in the space where the luggage ought to be.

18

SAMPSON began to wail, on a sing-song note, and to wring his hands and roll his eyes. Martin put a hand on the Negro's shoulder and pressed with empty reassurance. Beads of sweat had gathered on the black forehead, and Sampson's lips were parted; all from shock.

Richard didn't move. He seemed more shocked than Martin, just stood with his hands clenched by his side and his lips set tightly together. He stared at the body as if it hypnotised him. Martin glanced at him and saw that all the colour had fled from his cheeks; that made his eyes a more startling blue.

" You know who he is, don't you? " Martin said.

His voice sounded normal, and surprised himself. He went forward and, without touching the body, peered at the face. The man's head was turned away. He was in a sitting position, with his knees up, one hand resting on the floor of the boot. The twist of his neck, turning the face away, made it look as if he were a wax figure, and the head had been turned to face the wrong way. He had fair, curly hair. His face was waxen white; there was no sign of injury to his cheeks or head. He had a profile that would have served a Greek god, and his name was Raymond Dunn.

" Don't you? " asked Martin, and turned to look at his brother.

Richard's expression shocked him, oddly enough, more than the discovery of Raymond Dunn's body. There was no real surprise about finding Raymond dead; the possibility had been there for some time, and he had acknowledged it without speaking of it to Richard. After one galvanising moment, he had settled down to

142

acceptance of what had happened. Sampson's wailing had stopped, and he was wiping his forehead and muttering a little; doubtless he was praying. In a few minutes Sampson would be back to normal, this wouldn't throw him out of his stride for long.

Richard was a different matter; he looked as pale as the dead man. He hadn't known Raymond well enough to be really affected, yet he was horrified.

He moistened his lips, as if he were gradually recovering, and groped for his cigarettes. Sampson saw his movement and, as if glad to do something normal, took out a book of matches and struck one; his hand was quivering as he held out the light; and the cigarette shook in Richard's mouth.

" It's—Raymond Dunn," he said hoarsely.

" I wonder how long he's been there? " said Martin. He had an unpleasant fluttering in his stomach; the question had made one thing apparent: the dead man had been in the boot of the car during their journey. If the key had fitted the lock they would have found him before they'd reached here.

" Someone else—must have had a key," Richard said hoarsely. " But what was Raymond doing here? Why did he come here? "

" We brought him."

" Eh? Nonsense! Don't be a fool," Richard said abruptly. " If you mean we drove from London with that——"

His voice trailed off.

" Afraid so," said Martin. " Blond Beauty had a nasty surprise packet for us. Pity we didn't discover it before we arrived. The Lord knows what Mother will have to say about this new visitor." His lips twisted wryly. " If I thought it would do any good, I'd drive off for a few miles and discover it on the road, but——"

" Can't we do that? " Richard looked at Sampson. " Sampson wouldn't——"

" No, we can't," said Martin, almost roughly. " That

143

would make him a liar when the police questioned him. We'll have to see it through. Sampson!"

He smiled easily at the Jamaican.

"Yassah?"

"Don't say a word about this to Cook, or any of the others, or the gardeners, do you understand? We shall have to send for the police, and mustn't talk about it until they've arrived."

"I understand, Massa Martin."

Martin closed the boot and locked it, took out his pen-knife and made a scratch on the key which fitted, then slipped them all into his pocket.

"We'll send these back later. Go and get yourself a nip of rum, Sampson, and keep away from Mrs. Fane until I've seen you again. Mr. Fane may send for you, so stay around the kitchen."

"Yas, sah, Mr. Martin, sah."

Sampson hurried off, flat-footed, head bent. Martin turned towards the front of the house, and Richard followed, still deathly pale. It wasn't until they reached the front door that Richard seemed to shake off the worst effect of the shock, and he stepped more briskly into the house.

"Nice job, to tell Gillian," he said. "I wonder how she is."

"The last time I asked, she was still asleep."

"She can't sleep much longer," Richard said.

Sunlight shone on the woodland scene opposite the front door, and made the hall look bright and imposing. Martin started for the stairs, and Richard turned towards the drawing-room.

"What——" began Martin.

"I need a snort of whisky, old chap."

Martin watched him go into the room, saw him pour himself out a generous nip, which he drank neat. Then he lit another cigarette, and gave a shaky laugh.

"You can be the detective, brother. I don't like discovering dead bodies."

144

" Not good. Like me to see Dad? "

" Oh, I'll come."

Richard glanced at the bottle as if wondering if a second drink would do him good, and then joined Martin. As they went upstairs, they could hear the typewriter clattering away. In their youth it had been a major crime to enter the study when Fane was typing; because it meant that he was putting all his tremendous power of concentration into his work. Martin didn't tap, but opened the door.

Fane, in his shirt-sleeves, a cigarette sticking out from his lips at a jaunty angle, one eye half-closed behind the horn-rimmed glasses, was hitting the typewriter as if his very life depended on it. Martin watched for a fascinated moment, and Richard didn't speak. Fane hadn't noticed the interruption and didn't see Martin push the door to. Then he reached the end of a page, ripped the paper out of the machine, and glanced up. He started violently; the cigarette dropped from his lips.

" Sorry," said Martin.

Fane gulped, and picked the cigarette from the desk.

" I didn't hear you." He straightened the pages of freshly typed manuscript carefully, and put his cigarette into a huge, covered-in ash-tray. A spiral of smoke rose from the ash-tray, from the previous cigarette. " I suppose this won't keep for half an hour."

" Sorry," said Martin again.

Fane glanced at Richard, frowned, and pushed his chair back.

" No, obviously it won't. Seen a ghost? "

" Yes," said Martin. " Raymond Dunn's—or rather, his corpse. In the back of the Buick. We couldn't unlock the boot yesterday. Sampson found us a key, and there it was. We're wondering if we ought to drive off and make the discovery somewhere else."

" Because of your mother? " Fane smiled faintly, his only reaction. He paused for a while before adding, " No, you needn't worry about that. She'll take this

145

much more calmly than she took your arm last night. When are you going to realise that if it's a big thing she always stands up to it well? Trifles annoy her. Mrs. Dunn will be the big difficulty, but she will have to know, anyhow. She's still asleep—Tucker must have given her something to make sure nothing would wake her. Sit down, Skip."

Richard sat on the arm of a chair.

"Why are you so worried?"

Fane lost no time getting to the point.

Richard said, "How did it get there? Who put it there? Who killed him? The police already think we know more than we've said. If they find the body in the back of our car, they're going to start thinking a lot more about the part we've been playing. And——" He shot a glance at Martin. "Oh, forget it!"

"Do you think the body was there before you left the garage?" asked Fane.

"Of course it was," said Martin.

"Why of course? Haven't you left the car unattended anywhere?"

"Well——"

"Let's get this straight," said Jonathan Fane, and stood up and went to the window. He could just see the back of the garage. "You picked the car up from the garage yesterday morning, I gather, soon after nine o'clock. When did you first find that you couldn't unlock the boot?"

"When we had the flat tyre. Richard went to get the tools, and the key wouldn't work." Martin began to fill his pipe. "I suppose it is just possible that the body could have been put in while we were at Guildford. It was parked in a side street for a while. And it was outside Number 17 Nye Street for some time, while we were all in the house. But no, that's fantastic."

"Did you see anyone?"

"We know we were watched," said Martin thoughtfully. "Garrett came—remember? And Barbara says

146

that we were watched by Robertson, too. It's a quiet street. I suppose someone *could* have driven up and pushed the body in, and—Richard, did you leave the keys in the car? "

" Eh? "

" When we were at Nye Street, where did you leave the keys? In the car? "

" I—well, yes," said Richard. He had a little colour now, and his voice was stronger. " I found them in the ignition when I went to take Barbara off on the fool's errand. Told myself I must remember to pocket them, otherwise I was inviting a car-thief to take it away. Good Lord! "

" So the men could have found the boot key on the ring, opened the boot, put the body inside, and then locked up and taken the key away. It would make sure you couldn't find the body very quickly." Fane's lips began to curve. " A very neat trick, but more likely on my typewriter than in fact."

" Screamingly funny," said Richard tartly.

Fane put his head on one side.

" No, just ingenious, if that's the way it happened. Did you leave the car anywhere else? "

" Outside the Crown Hotel, Blandford, while we had dinner," said Martin. " I don't think anything could have been done there. No one could have guessed where we were going to stop, and the spot where we had to park was practically on the road. Traffic was passing within a few feet of it all the time. It's near a corner, and the lighting's pretty good."

" That seems conclusive," said Fane. He turned and picked up the telephone, which stood on the window-ledge, pressed a little button on it, and then said, " Miss Wilkinson, see if you can get Inspector Medley for me, will you. . . . Put him through straight away and tell him it's urgent." He put the telephone down, smiled again, and said almost casually, " You two haven't any idea who did this, have you? "

Martin smiled.

Richard flushed.

" Look here——"

" Medley will wonder and eventually ask. I'd rather know the whole truth before he does, if there's anything to know. I'm not suggesting that you murdered the fellow," Fane added, chuckling. " On the other hand, you might possibly have concealed the body, in defence of someone whose innocence you believe in."

" We don't belong to the school of romantic mystery," said Richard.

" You know nothing you haven't already told me? "

" Not a thing," said Richard, and forced a laugh. " Sorry if I snapped at you. I don't mind admitting that when I saw the body I had the nastiest shock of my life. I've never been happy about corpses."

" I know the feeling," Fane went on in the same casual voice. " Not taking big risks by defending Barbara Marrison, Scoop, are you? "

Martin's gaze was very direct.

" No, Dad."

" Good. You realise that she may be mixed up in this, don't you? "

" Unhappily, yes."

That came slowly.

" Had you ever seen or heard of her before yesterday? "

" No."

" That also goes for me," said Richard. " Believe it or not, your favourite sons are quite innocent." He seemed to have fully recovered. " I think——"

The telephone bell rang.

" Yes," said Fane, and listened, nodded, and said, " I see, thanks." He put the receiver down. " Medley's on his way here, he might be here at any minute. He'll be in complete charge, of course, and if his questions get a bit personal I shouldn't fly off the handle at him. Policemen get suspicious of quick tempers when murder investigations are on the go. He rang up earlier this morning, by the way, and told me he was getting in touch with Scotland Yard, so we may have a visitor from there, too."

As he finished, he heard a car turn into the drive, looked out, and said:

" Here's Medley already. I'll go and have a word with him. You stay up here, will you? "

He went out briskly, a burly and self-confident figure, and a draught coming from the window stirred the grey hair, which was untidy and looked more than ever in need of cutting. Richard pushed his hand through his own hair, and said ruefully:

" He'd make a good magistrate, wouldn't he? "

" He's still a hard man to lie to," said Martin. " I'm glad we're not lying. Are we? "

He looked into Richard's eyes, and was smiling mildly, but there was no doubt of the implication in the question. Richard didn't try to evade the challenge in his eyes. He didn't speak immediately, but his lips began to curve; Martin found that a relief. They heard voices downstairs, which faded quickly; so Fane had taken the detective into another room for a preliminary talk. Richard stood up, stubbed out his cigarette, and immediately lit another.

" No, Scoop, we're not lying. I'm suffering from shock effect—much as I was last night. Can you take it straight? "

" Let's have it."

" Your pal Garrett wasn't watching the house while we were there, or after I'd taken Barbara off. If he had been, he wouldn't have broken in so gaily, knowing you were still about. You said that he was—that was what the Maestro would call a half-lie. On the other hand, Barbara and Robertson were obviously interested in Dunn's house. It's much more likely that Barbara's crowd know something about it. I don't, personally, believe this story. Sorry. I was inclined to, at first, but I don't think I've misjudged Barbara as a woman.

She would take some knowing, and she wouldn't be easy with her favours. Her story about searching your room for the diamonds and all that blah struck me as being highly improbable. I'd even say that she melted, so to speak, because she wanted to make sure you didn't make a fuss about her early morning visit. She wanted to be free to skip during the night. Not good, Martin. Sorry."

Martin didn't speak.

" Of course, I could be wrong about part of it," Richard said. " Believe it or not, I don't want Barbara to turn out a bad 'un. I've a feeling that she hit you like a sledgehammer, emotionally speaking."

" I see," said Martin. " Thanks for the frankness, anyhow."

He turned to the window, thrust his hands deep into his pockets, and stared out. He was still staring out when footsteps drew near and the door opened. He turned, to see Medley, who looked bulkier and darker by day than he had by night, and whose face was florid and whose eyes were nearly as blue as Richard's, although not so large. Fane came just behind him. Medley held a wash-leather bag in his hand, and switched their thoughts immediately from the body to the diamonds.

" So you've got them," Martin said equably.

" Yes, Mr. Fane, we've got them," said Medley.

" They're paste," said Jonathan Fane simply. " There isn't a real diamond among them."

There was a long, tense pause; then Medley broke it.

" What did you do with the real ones? " he asked as if he were asking the time of day.

RICHARD said explosively, "Don't be a fool!" and clenched his hands. Martin didn't move. Medley stared at him, as if accusingly. Jonathan Fane watched without showing any expression, and his eyes were very steady. Martin returned the detective's stare, without any sign of emotion, and the tone of his voice was quite amiable.

"They're the things I took from that deed-box."

"Can you prove it, Mr. Fane?"

"No. I opened the box myself, no one else knew anything about it until I told Richard when we were on the road. I needn't have told him. I needn't have told you. If I'd knowingly put paste diamonds into the bank's safe, I needn't have let on to anyone. Or don't you agree?"

Medley didn't answer.

"It stands to reason," Richard said hotly.

"Possibly," said Medley. "Mr. Fane, I'm asking you again—did you put the real diamonds somewhere else?"

"If those aren't real, I've never seen the real ones."

"Thank you." That might have meant anything. Medley shifted his position, and Jonathan Fane pushed past him, but didn't sit down and didn't ask the detective to sit. Medley dropped the wash-leather bag into his pocket, and coughed. "When did you last see Raymond Dunn?"

"Several weeks ago."

"Can't you be more precise?"

"No. We went round to Pete Dunn's flat one evening,

he threw a little party once a month or so, and Raymond was there."

"What about you?" asked Medley, turning to Richard.

"The same applies."

"I see, thanks. I think we'll go and look at the body," said Medley. .

"Want me?" asked Martin.

"No, thank you, but I want the key of the boot."

Martin handed the bunch over, explaining the mark, and Medley turned and went out, nodding vaguely; he plodded as he walked, and Richard threw his hands up in the air, as if in exasperation. Medley had shown as much animation as a waxen figure. They heard him plodding down the stairs, and Richard said:

"There goes someone's doom."

"Don't under-rate Medley," said Jonathan Fane briskly. "He seems slow, but he's good. Get your own position clear in your minds, too. Scoop, I know it's nonsense, but if I were standing outside this and being quite dispassionate, I'd think along the same lines as Medley. That you might have been in this game for some time, and faked diamonds ready for a switch, found the real diamonds and hid them, and put the fakes in their place. It would be a pretty clever trick. You could tell the story you've told, it would appear to stand up, it would be extremely difficult to prove anything against you, although there would be plenty of suspicion. Medley knows that Miss Marrison and Robertson also suspect you, and——"

"So now the police are sitting up and taking notice when a couple of phoney private detectives——"

"They're not phoney," said Jonathan Fane, and smiled; his eyes were gleaming as he looked at Martin. "They're genuine. Everything they told us about themselves is true. They work for Relvon—Miss Marrison is directly employed by the company, and Robertson's agency has been hired by Relvon, at Miss Marrison's request."

Martin didn't speak, but the shadows went out of his eyes.

.   .   .   .   .

Barbara had not lied.

She thought that she had reason to suspect him of complicity; she hadn't, and that would eventually be proved, so it didn't matter. Until then he had been feeling heavy-hearted and miserable. Nothing had affected him so much as Barbara's disappearance and the indication that she had lied. The rest hardly mattered. Medley could suspect as much as he liked, they could even be suspected of knowing about Raymond Dunn's body, but——

He chuckled, for the first time that day.

.   .   .   .   .

" My relations have the oddest sense of humour," Richard said explosively. " Barbara pulls a fast one, we put ourselves in line for suspicion of murder and robbery, and it's something to laugh about. Especially for Scoop! Medley tells him to his face that he switched those diamonds. The attack on the road makes it pretty sure that Smart Rummy assumed that he did. It's still funny. Odd, how you can live with a man for twenty-five years and not really get to know him."

Jonathan Fane said easily, " Wait until you start living with a woman! " He went to his desk, sat down, ran his fingers through the pages of the half-finished book on which he was working, and chuckled; it was when he and Martin were laughing, like that, that the likeness between them became so noticeable. " I couldn't have thought up a better one myself! I'll bet a signed copy of this book to dinner in town that I'll find the explanation before either of you."

" Sharing clues? " asked Richard.

" Oh, yes."

" And forming our own conclusions," said Martin, still in a much sunnier mood. " It's on. First clue: Barbara vanished last night. What's your conclusion? "

" Don't get confused between conclusions and guesses,"
said Jonathan Fane. " My guess is that she decided,
after all, that you were as honest as you look, and wanted
to get somewhere else in a hurry."

" Why not leave a note of explanation? " asked
Richard.

" She hadn't much time. It would have been wasting
time to write, anyhow." He glanced at the door, which
opened silently; only Sampson could approach and open
a door without giving warning of his approach. " Hallo,
Sampson! I'm told you had a nasty surprise this
morning."

" Yes, sah! " said Sampson fervently. " I doan' want
more shocks ob dat kind, Massa Fane. That Massa
Medley is looking at de body right now, sah. I doan'
t'ink I like Massa Medley. De postman hab just brought
dis," Sampson added, and laid down a parcel, obviously
of books, and a letter. " De letter's fo' yo', Massa
Martin."

Martin said in surprise, " For me? No one knows I'm
here."

" I can read," said Sampson with simple pride.

The letter was in a pale-blue envelope and addressed in
a bold hand to Martin Fane, Esquire; it had been posted
in Dorchester, and had obviously caught the early morning
post. He opened it quickly. Fane was cutting the
string round his parcel, but glanced up at Martin before
he took the brown paper off. Richard, quick to see the
possibilities, went to Martin's side.

" Mind if I look? "

Martin didn't speak, but read:

" Martin, I'm terribly sorry I had to leave in such
a hurry. I'll explain later. Please thank your
mother and father for their hospitality, I do hope
they'll forgive me. And please—be careful, don't
meddle in this affair.

Barbara."

"Is that what I think it is?" asked Fane.

Richard grinned, and Sampson looked delighted.

"It is! A nice polite little note from Barbara, which means that Martin will now be convinced that she couldn't have a mean thought about him. She's going to explain later, but how she'll explain having to get up in the middle of the night and flit, I don't know. Women are always wonderful, though."

Martin handed the note to his father.

"Nice of her," Fane remarked, after reading.

"Oh, she's delightful," said Richard. "Just a trifle sphinx-like, that's all. I wonder what the great detective is doing. Did he telephone for more supporters, Dad?"

"Yes. His photographers and finger-print men will be here at any time," said Fane. "Sampson, let me know the moment Mrs. Fane arrives, I want to see her—stay in the garden and tell me as soon as her car turns in at the gates, will you?"

"Yassa."

Sampson went off, grinning broadly. A job which entailed sitting and watching was his constant dream.

   .   .   .   .   .

Medley's men arrived from Dorchester before Evelyn Fane returned. Martin and Richard watched them, from a distance, taking photographs, testing the boot for finger-prints, and taking out the body. It was still stiff; when they had it out of the boot, it was in almost the same position as it had been inside. A police-surgeon had come with the second group of policemen, and they watched him examine the body; he gave particular attention to the head and neck. As far as they could see, the only outward sign of injury was the curious position of the head. More photographs were taken, and then an ambulance arrived, and the body was transferred to it. The police talked quietly, the Fane brothers caught only an occasional word. Jonathan Fane had stayed in the study; they could hear the typewriter going.

Sampson kept his distance from the police, and watched the drive gates.

They had heard Medley telephone Dr. Tucker about Gillian Dunn, and gathered that Tucker wanted her to wake naturally. The police-surgeon and Medley looked into her room but made no attempt to disturb her.

The brothers became tired of watching.

" It's getting late, isn't it? " Martin asked, and glanced at his watch. " One-fifteen, Mother's usually back for a prompt one-o'clock lunch."

" They're waylaying her in the village with floods of questions," said Richard. " I'll tell you one thing, this will mean publicity with a capital P. Funny, I hadn't thought of it before. The Maestro will find his sales shoot up with a bump, especially if he happens to solve the mystery. It wouldn't surprise me at all that, either, I'd put my money on him rather than Medley. Let's go in and have a quick one before lunch."

They strolled towards the house.

Medley followed, and they entered the hall together.

Jonathan Fane was coming downstairs, his hair awry, his forehead wrinkled; he was more worried now than he had been all morning.

" Mother not back yet? "

" No," said Martin.

" I expected her back well before one. Anything more I can do for you, Inspector? "

" I don't think so, Mr. Fane, thanks." Medley still put as much feeling into his words as an automaton might. " I'll have to take the Buick away with me, of course, and I'd like your sons to make formal statements now, then come into Dorchester this afternoon, if they will, and sign their statements. I'll have them typed out and ready by half-past five. Mind you," he added slowly, " I could bring them in, but if it would be no trouble——"

" We'll come," Martin said.

" Thank you. Where did you say you bought the car? "

"Percy Mellor's, Gilling Street, Paddington. It's off Praed Street," Martin said. "Mellor will tell you that everything we've told you about it is true."

"Oh, I'm sure."

"For that matter, so will Tom Rowbottom," said Richard. "We've lashings of evidence, Inspector."

"That's good," said Medley heavily. "Let me have all the keys of the car, will you?"

"There goes our hope of three weeks' tour of the British Isles," said Richard, handing over the keys. "Be careful with her, she's precious. I shall sue you if there's as much as a scratch on her beautiful body."

"We won't damage the car," said Medley.

They made brief statements which a plain-clothes man took down in shorthand, then Medley went off.

The three Fanes watched until he disappeared on the way to the garage. Fane turned into the drawing-room.

"You two had better have a drink," he said. "Pour me out a tomato juice, will you?" He glanced at an ornamental gilt clock, which was on the wall over a china-cabinet filled with fragile-looking blue-and-gold china. "I wish your mother would come back."

Richard went to the cocktail cabinet.

"Where was she going?" asked Martin.

"She had to see some women about a garden fête next month. She didn't want to go, but I persuaded her that she couldn't do anything useful here."

Richard came towards him with the tomato juice. He sipped it, then put down the glass and went across to the telephone. He gave a Lichen Abbas number, and stood with his back to the room, looking towards the drive. Sampson was still watching; it was half-past one.

"Hallo. . . . Is that Mrs. Richardson?" Fane spoke quietly into the mouthpiece. "It's Jonathan Fane here. Has my wife left yet?"

He paused; and his fingers seemed to tighten on the telephone. Richard tossed down his drink, Martin frowned.

" *What* time? " asked Fane. " I see—thanks very much. She didn't say she was going on anywhere else, did she? . . . Oh, no, it can't be anything serious. Thanks very much, good-bye."

He put down the receiver, and now he looked really worried.

" She left at five past twelve, and said she was coming straight back. That makes her nearly an hour and a half late. There can't have been an accident on the road."

" The police have been going to and fro all the morning," Richard said slowly. " Even Medley would see if there'd been a smash. She probably stopped off at a house *en route* and was persuaded to dally. We know how these women talk."

" Do we? " asked Fane. He lifted the telephone and dialled another number and was connected immediately. " Hallo, Vicar—Fane here. Has my wife called this morning? . . . Thanks. No, nothing to worry about." He put the receiver down heavily, paused, and then dialled again. " Mrs. Forsythe? Fane here. Has my wife? . . ."

He made seven calls; the answer was the same in each case. By the time he had finished it was nearly two o'clock. He beckoned Sampson in from the garden; it was like him to say nothing to the others until Sampson had arrived and been sent to tell cook to serve lunch at once.

Sampson went off.

" I don't like this," Richard said softly.

Fane didn't speak, but lifted the telephone again and called the Dorchester Police. Medley wasn't in. Fane wouldn't speak to anyone else, but dialled Medley's home number.

" Hallo, Medley—Fane here. My wife should have been home just after twelve, and hasn't turned up yet. I've inquired at every shop and house in the village where she might have called. She was last seen leaving the village, at ten past twelve, driving her Standard Twelve.

158

It's most unlike her to be late. Sorry to add to your worries, but will you have inquiries made. . . . Eh? . . . Well, it's just possible there was an accident and someone took her into the hospital, I suppose, but it isn't likely. . . . Did you have any men in the village this morning? . . . No, I suppose there wasn't any reason. . . . Yes, I'll be glad if you will, I'm really worried about her. Thanks."

He rang off.

" I'm going down to the village to have a look round," Richard said. " Someone must have seen her——"

" She isn't in the village," said Fane slowly. " Old Patterson was in his garden when she passed, coming this way. It's the last house between the village and here, so she was on the way. I don't think there's any point in leaving until we've had some lunch. Or until we get word." He was frowning, almost scowling. " It isn't conceivable that——"

He broke off.

Richard said softly, " It *is* conceivable that Smart Rummy thought it would be a good idea if he kidnapped her, isn't it? He couldn't think of a better way of making us cough up the diamonds, and he certainly thinks we have them."

Fane didn't speak.

" Damn it——" began Martin, and broke off.

" *I'm* going to the village," said Richard. " Never mind food."

He hurried out of the room. Fane hesitated, and Martin went to the door, talking as he moved.

" I think he's right, Dad. It's worth having a look round right away. I can't believe that Richard's right, but if he should be, the quicker we know the better."

" All right," said his father.

.   .   .   .   .

Near a corner about three-quarters of a mile from Nairn Lodge they saw skid marks on the road, where a car had pulled up quickly, and then the imprints of tyres in the soft earth at the side of the road, washed there by r cent heavy rains. Fane was sure they were the tracks of the Standard Twelve. Men's footsteps were dotted about; so were a woman's. The tyre marks of a larger car showed, not far from those of the Standard.

. . . . .

"Yes," said Fane into the telephone. "There isn't much doubt about it. She was held up on the road and forced to get into another car. Her own car was driven off, and well—you have the number. . . . Thanks. . . . Yes, if I get any word, I'll let you know at once. Thanks, Inspector." He put the receiver down slowly, and looked across at his sons. His face was set, and there was a glint in his eyes which they seldom saw. He looked older; he also looked as if he were savagely angry and was trying to fight against showing it. He said, "If either of you boys has left out a tiny detail, tell me."

His voice was low-pitched, and quivering slightly.

"Nothing."

They spoke together.

"Right! Richard, I'm going to Guildford and London, and want you to come with me. I'm going to this house in Nye Street first, and then to the garage where you bought the car. Don't tell Medley that, if he inquires, Martin. I want you to stay here, and I'll telephone along the road, you can tell me if you'd had any word. Meanwhile, call up your Fleet Street friends and tell them the story. They can get photographs of your Mother from Tenby, my agent—give them Tenby's number, Whitehall 89511. If this man Rummy telephones, as he may, tell him you'll pass on a message. *Don't* do anything he asks, that would only make matters worse."

Richard was already at the door.

"If anything happens to her, I'll never forgive myself," Martin said in a shocked voice.

"I know. Keep your head."

Fane turned and hurried out of the drawing-room.

The Humber, a powerful black limousine, had turned out of the drive, watched by Sampson and the gardener from the grounds and by Martin at the window, when the telephone bell rang.

20

MARTIN kept his voice very low.

" This is Lichen Abbas double-three."

" Hold on, please, I have a London call for you."

The operator's voice faded. Martin held on, with the receiver pressed close against his ear, and his teeth set; his hand hurt, because he gripped so hard. He stared at a picture, the middle of three on the fireplace wall; of a prim, pale beauty with creamy shoulders and a deep red wrap, painted so well that it looked as if the velvet were real; it was his mother's favourite picture.

There were odd sounds on the line.

" Here you are, caller, you're through," said the operator, and a man said urgently:

" Hallo, hallo! Mr. Fane there? "

The voice was familiar; it wasn't Smart Rummy's; or at least not the voice of the leader of the gang which had held the Buick up on the road. It was Barbara's friend, Robertson.

" Martin Fane speaking."

" Martin? Oh, yes. Is Barbara there? "

Martin didn't answer.

" Is she there? " Robertson bellowed into the telephone, and he seemed as if he might be dancing with rage. " Is Barbara there? "

" No."

" Are you sure? It's important. She was supposed to be back here an hour ago, and she's not come. I don't know where she is. Has she phoned you to-day? Have you any idea where she is? "

" No," said Martin.

" Well, if you hear from her, tell her to call me at the

162

office at once. It's urgent—make her do it at once, do you understand? "

" Yes. But what——"

" I can't explain over the phone. We made a discovery this morning that might——"

He broke off. Martin heard him catch his breath, and wondered if it were as ominous as it sounded. There wasn't another sound for several seconds—then the telephone clattered and a man shouted. Martin held on to the instrument tightly, and his knuckles went white. The telephone clattered on to something hard, and then there was silence, followed by another shout—and a ringing echo of a shot. It was so loud that it almost deafened him; he snatched the telephone away from his ear. He put it to the other side, but his ears were ringing, he couldn't be sure that he really heard anything else, until the receiver was banged back on its cradle.

Martin's forehead was damp and cold; his neck felt stiff. He put down the receiver and waited tensely for a few seconds, then picked it up. He refused to let himself panic.

" Dorchester police-station," he said.

" Just a moment, please."

As he waited, he moved his left arm and took out a small pocket diary, turned the pages over with some difficulty and then came to the list of telephone numbers. He pressed a finger-nail against the name of Rowbottom, who had a Central number.

" Dorchester police-station."

" Inspector Medley, please."

" I'm sorry, sir, he's not in."

" Anyone who can take shorthand notes. This is Martin Fane."

" Just a moment, sir."

Moments seemed to take an age; and this was desperately urgent.

" Ready, sir, carry on," said another man crisply.

" This is Martin Fane, of Lichen Abbas. I was speaking on the telephone to Mr. Robertson, of the Robertson Inquiry Agency, in London—three or four minutes ago. I heard a shot in the office. The receiver was then replaced. You'll know what to do."

" Do you know the address, sir? "

" No. Inspector Medley will know something about it. Good-bye." Martin rang off, paused again while staring at the pert eyes of the woman in the picture, and then lifted the telephone. " I want a trunk call, please, to Central 85185. My number is Lichen Abbas 33. I'll hold on."

He held on, and felt the clamminess at his forehead spread to his neck. Outside, the scene was so quiet and peaceful, the gardener still worked on the flower-beds, bees hummed against the window from the riot of flowers in the bed just outside.

" *Daily Echo*, can I help you? "

" Mr. Rowbottom, please."

" One moment, sir."

That seemed all anyone could say: one moment, sir. Added together, the moments made minutes which might be precious. His mother had been kidnapped. That was the simple truth of it; kidnapped because he had been so damned smart in breaking open that deed-box. He gritted his teeth. The moments passed; Tom might not be in, he was possibly out with the car, but early afternoon was his usual time for being at the desk.

" Hallo? "

He was in.

" Tom, listen. It's Martin here. My mother has been kidnapped, and I shall probably hear from the kidnapper soon. I can't leave here. My father and Richard have gone to London, they're going to see Percy Mellor. Raymond Dunn's body was found in the back of that Buick, and father obviously thinks it might have been put in at Mellor's garage. I don't. He's anxious the police shouldn't know they've gone to town. You can judge whether they should."

He paused.

" Yes, I've all that," said Rowbottom very steadily.

" Next. A shot was fired, ten minutes ago, in the office of a man named Robertson of the Robertson Inquiry Agency. I've told the police. I don't know what happened, but I should think Robertson was shot."

" Yes, old chap," said Rowbottom calmly.

" That's all."

" Want publicity? "

" If you'll give me your news desk——"

" No, give it to an Agency," said Rowbottom. " The *Echo* will want to scoop it, and an Agency will get it into every evening paper to-night. You'd better call them, I've enough to do. Central 21212, and ask for Freddy Stanner—you know him."

" Yes. Thanks, Tom."

" Glad I was in," said Rowbottom briefly. " Martin, be very careful. I've been making inquiries, and this is a nasty job. A man named Rummy is at the back of it. He's dangerous. No one knows exactly who he is, but they know he's as bad as they come."

" Thanks."

" Has that Dunn woman talked yet? " asked Rowbottom abruptly.

" No."

" Does she know that her husband's dead? "

" I don't think so. The police may have told her, but the last I heard she was still sleeping under a drug the doctor gave her last night."

" Tackle her," said Rowbottom. " My opinion yesterday was that she knew a lot and had a nasty conscience. It wasn't just anxiety for her husband. 'Bye."

He rang off, and Martin put down the receiver and looked at the door. Medley may have seen Gillian; he hadn't worried about her, hadn't given her any thought. He moved towards the door, and then picked up the receiver again.

Freddy Stanner of the Central Agency was in; and

took the message with much more excitement than Rowbottom had shown, but he didn't waste any time.

Martin heard a car, as he finished talking. His heart leapt. His mother? He stood rigid, staring at the drive, as the car turned in at the gate; it wasn't the Standard. It was a Wolseley, sleek and modern, and he recognised Dr. Tucker at the wheel. He was absurdly disappointed —and he wanted to see Gillian himself, before anyone else spoke to her. He hurried out of the room and up the stairs, reached the door of the spare room, and turned the handle.

The room was gloomy, because the blinds were drawn. It was large; the best bedroom in the house, Evelyn Fane made sure that her guests were well impressed; he had been surprised when he had learned that Gillian had been put in here. There was a large double bed, and he saw Gillian's dark hair on the pillow, jet black— the white of the pillow-case and of her face made it seem even more black and luxuriant than he had realised before.

He closed the door softly and stepped across to her. His footsteps were muffled by the carpet. He couldn't hear her breathing; she must have gone under pretty completely to Tucker's drug. Would it be safe to wake her now? He stood looking down. She had an almost alarming pallor; like Raymond's.

He said quietly, " Gillian."

She didn't stir.

" Gillian, wake up."

He didn't know anything about the effect of drugs; it might be a bad thing to disturb her, and even dangerous. He touched her shoulder, and it was cool. She didn't make the slightest movement.

" Gillian," he said more loudly, and shook her gently.

There wasn't any sign of life, and a stab of fear entered his mind. He tried to fight it off. He stood back, staring at her. He heard footsteps outside, and there was a tap at the door. He didn't answer. The girl on the bed didn't seem to be breathing, there was no movement

166

at her lips, and her pallor made her face look like wax.

There was no more tapping at the door.

He swung round and strode towards it, opened it, and went out on to the landing. Half-way down the stairs was one of the maids, she glanced up over her shoulder. Tucker stood in the hall at the foot of the stairs, hat in hand, carrying his bright yellow pigskin bag.

" Hallo, Martin! "

" She didn't answer, sir," said the maid.

" All right, Ethel," said Martin, and the girl went to the kitchen. " Hallo, Doc."

" What the devil's the matter with you? " asked Tucker, and stared into Martin's set face. " You look ready to drop."

" Come upstairs, will you? " asked Martin heavily. " I've just been in to see Mrs. Dunn, and don't like the look of her."

" Oh, she's all right," said Tucker breezily; he was so boyish that it was hard to believe that he could make a satisfactory doctor. " What's all this about your mother? I'm told in the village that you've been telephoning all over the place, and she's missing or something."

" Yes."

Tucker stopped at the head of the stairs.

" You're not serious."

" Aren't I? " said Martin heavily.

He moved towards the bedroom door, which he had left ajar. Tucker strode in, frowned at the windows, and went straight to the bed.

" Let's have some daylight, old chap."

Martin drew the curtains. Tucker stood by the side of the bed, looking at Gillian Dunn much as Richard had stared at her husband a few hours earlier. He didn't speak. Martin moved slowly towards him, but knew exactly what was passing through his mind; felt sure that the girl was dead.

.   .   .   .

The body was still warm. She hadn't been dead many hours, in Tucker's opinion. Her eyes, with their pin-point pupils, told him that she had died from morphine poisoning; he hadn't given her morphine.

.   .   .   .   .

" Don't touch anything and don't do anything," Tucker said. " I'll telephone the police. Tell them exactly what you told me. Martin! Can you hear me? "

" Er—yes. Yes, of course."

" Go downstairs and give yourself a strong whisky," Tucker advised.

He watched Martin walk down the stairs, without looking back, and then glanced round at the dead girl on the bed. He rubbed his chin very slowly, hesitated, and went to the small room next to the study. In there, a tall, lanky girl with straight hair and a prominent nose was working on some manuscripts; she had a remarkably neat handwriting, and Tucker knew that her speed on a typewriter was phenomenal. She glanced up, and took off her pale-coloured glasses.

" Good afternoon, Doctor."

" Good afternoon, Miss Wilkinson. You know that Mr. Fane probably won't be back to-day, don't you? "

" Oh, yes, but I've plenty of work to do."

" I'm sure," said Tucker, and grinned faintly. " I wonder if you'll go outside to my car, and bring me in the small case, you'll find it on the back seat."

" *Gladly*, doctor."

" Thanks. Then go into the kitchen—before you bring the case to me—and ask them to put on a kettle of water. Bring the water up when it's boiled, will you? "

" Ethel can——" began Miss Wilkinson.

" I'd rather you brought it up," said Tucker. " You can make sure it's put into a clean bowl for me."

" *Very* good," said Miss Wilkinson.

As soon as she had gone Tucker went into the study where, he knew, Fane had a line direct to the exchange which had no extension except to his secretary's room.

Tucker called the Dorchester Police-station; Medley was in.

"Tucker here," said Tucker, and stopped looking like a schoolboy. "I'm at Jonathan Fane's house. The woman who came here yesterday is dead." He paused to listen. "Yes, I'm sure," he went on grimly. "Also, she died from morphine poisoning which she certainly took while she was here. Fane and his younger son have gone off somewhere, the other son is still here. He found the body. I thought you ought to know at once. There's obviously grave trouble in the family, although I don't know much about it. I've sent Fane's secretary out so that I could tell you this without being overheard. Is there anything I can do while I'm here?"

"Lock that door and keep the key," said Medley promptly. "And wait——"

"I can't stay until you arrive, I've an urgent call in the village."

"Where?"

"The baker's—Tidworth's."

"Leave the key for me there, in an envelope," said Medley. "I'll get along just as soon as I can. Tell Fane to wait for me."

He rang off without another word.

Tucker went back to the spare bedroom, and was looking at the dead girl when Miss Wilkinson came up the stairs. He took the water and the small case at the door, and went into the room again, rejecting the girl's offer of help. When she was safely in her office he came out, locked the door, and went downstairs.

Martin was standing at the window, looking down the drive; he did not appear to have taken the advice about the whisky. Obviously he was waiting for someone to arrive. He started when Tucker entered the room.

"Hallo."

"Medley will come out as soon as he can," said Tucker. "He'd like you to wait here for him."

"I see. Thanks."

169

" Had that pick-me-up? "

" I don't need a pick-me-up," said Martin, and gave a slow smile. " I'll be all right, thanks."

Tucker was frowning when he went out, and twice looked back as he drove towards the gates. Martin Fane hadn't moved. Everything in the grounds seemed normal. The Jamaican was near the gates; he waved and gave his broad, cheerful smile.

Tucker drove on to his urgent case, and left the key in the baker's shop before he went upstairs.

. . . . .

It was half-past four. Martin had not heard from the police, although he'd expected them within half an hour of Tucker's going. For local police they probably had more than they could easily cope with at short notice. He had heard nothing from London, had no word of any kind. His thoughts shifted from one thing to another; the worst was his own share of the responsibility for what had happened here. He'd been so anxious to help Pete Dunn that he had taken wild risks; Richard had seen the possibility before he had; Richard was always quicker on the uptake.

He thought of the diamonds; and the anxiety of Gillian Dunn; and the fact that she had died of poisoning, in this house. It was an ugly thought, and would probably increase the police suspicion; he didn't need telling what would be suspected—that someone here had killed her. It wasn't one of the family; he knew that, even if the police took it for granted that it was.

It was possible that Barbara Marrison had drugged her; Barbara, or Robertson?

He could imagine the sound of that shot going off in Robertson's office. Robertson hadn't said a word to give him a clue about the person who must have entered the office—the man or woman. He'd just broken off, as if in alarm—the telephone had fallen, and the shot had followed.

Where was Barbara?

Martin's thoughts switched again to his mother. He could imagine what had happened; she had been held up on a corner and forced to get out, and she hadn't had a chance. Had the man named Rummy kidnapped her?

Was there any sense in his father's rush to Guildford and London?

Could Gillian Dunn have told him more than she had?

Could Barbara?

It was twenty-five minutes to five; he seemed to be looking at his watch every few minutes. He kept glancing at the telephone, too, expecting it to ring; the line seemed to be dead. Only this morning his father had been writing furiously about such a mystery as this; of murder and crime, and probably kidnapping. He recalled the way his father had looked when he had realised what had happened to his wife.

The telephone bell rang, at a moment when he wasn't expecting it. He went across to it.

" Lichen Abbas 33."

" *Martin*," said Barbara Marrison.

21

" HALLO, who's that? "

Martin kept his voice low, and tried to sound as if he hadn't the slightest idea who it was.

" Martin, that is you, isn't it? This is Barbara."

" Barbara! "

He hoped the note of surprise sounded convincing.

" Yes. Martin, your mother——"

"What do you know about her? " He barked the words. "What the hell are you playing at? Where is she? "

" Martin, be quiet and listen. I don't know where she is, but I know she's been kidnapped. I think I'm on the right track, but I've got to move quickly. I'm going to 31 Morden Street, Chelsea. Have you got that? I'll ring again as soon as I've found anything more. If you don't hear from me, tell the police where I've gone."

" But—— "

" Trust me," said Barbara urgently. " Never mind what others say or you think, trust me."

She rang off.

He knew she had, although he said " Hallo " several times, and was reluctant to put the receiver down. He didn't move.

Last night she had believed that he had the diamonds; so had Smart Rummy. Last night she had burgled his room, and there was no doubt that if she had found the diamonds she would have gone off without a word. Although his father had been assured that she worked for the insurance company, that did not make it certain that she was not also working with the thieves. He dare not trust his own judgment of her. She had believed that he had the diamonds, and wanted them desperately. So did others, who were prepared to kidnap and to kill in order to get them.

Barbara might be working with those other people; and might have rung him up then in the hope that he would go to the house in Morden Street—and walk into a trap. She couldn't have put out a more cunning bait. She knew he wouldn't go to the police.

The telephone bell rang again. He lifted the receiver quickly.

" Lichen Abbas 33."

" Just a moment, please, I have a call for you," said the girl.

More moments! He looked stonily out of the window, half-expecting to hear his father. Instead, it was a man whose voice was only vaguely familiar.

" Is that Mr. Fane? "

" Martin Fane speaking."

" *Good* afternoon," said the man, and Martin recognised his voice; it was the man of the hold-up. " We met last night, you may remember. Since then, I've had the pleasure of meeting your mother. You have some little things that I'm anxious to get, and I am calling to ask you to do nothing with them until you hear from me again. Good-bye."

He rang off abruptly.

   .   .   .   .   .

Medley had been a surprisingly long time coming to see the body of Gillian Dunn, and surely wouldn't be much longer. When he arrived there would be the interminable questions. He would want to know where Richard and his father had gone, and wouldn't take evasive answers well. Tucker had been shocked by the death of the girl, it had taken him completely by surprise; he'd talked about morphine, and the closer Martin thought over what he'd said, the more obvious it seemed that the doctor believed that the poison had been administered while Gillian had been at Nairn Lodge. In any case, that was pretty obvious.

He found his lips curving wryly; at least he was beginning to think again. He had to think to some purpose.

No matter how much he wanted to believe that Barbara's message was genuine, only a fool would ignore the possibility of a trap. Robertson was probably dead. Richard and his father might be running into trouble; they probably were. He had never seen his father in such a mood; he would take any risks for his wife.

Martin's smile disappeared, his lips set tightly.

His only chance of getting at the truth was through Barbara. Unless he saw her, he would hang around here, getting furious with the police. In his present mood he certainly wouldn't be able to stand Medley's manner. He fancied that Medley had soft-pedalled, so far, because of his respect for Jonathan Fane. Without that restraining influence the detective would probably step up the pressure. Looked at coldly, Medley had plenty of grounds for thinking that the Fane brothers were concerned with the murders and the disappearance of the diamonds.

Martin began to smile again.

He went out of the room and up to his bedroom. He'd forgotten one trifle which Medley hadn't suspected. He still had the automatic pistol which he had taken from Garrett at Nye Street; he'd slipped it under some clothes on a wardrobe shelf. He took it out and opened it; the gun still had four bullets. He'd handled a similar type of weapon before. He made sure that the safety catch was on, and slipped it into his right-hand pocket.

He hurried past the room where Gillian lay, glancing at the door. His stomach was painful when he moved quickly, and his left arm stiff, but he wasn't by any means incapacitated.

He went out by a side door, near the empty garage, where Sampson was busy mending a puncture in his bicycle tyre. He had practically finished, and was tightening the wheel bolts. He stood up when Martin appeared, and his broad smile did not conceal his anxiety

174

" Any news from de massa, sah? "

" Not yet, Sampson, but he'll be all right. Where did you say they had a Buick? "

" *Your* car, Massa Martin? De police——"

" No. There was one at a garage somewhere near, where you went for the keys."

" Dat's right," said Sampson, brightening. " But dey had only two keys, I went into Dorchester to get some mo'. Seemed a fool thing fo' me not to do dat, sah, and I sho' tried plenty hard. If I had known what was in dat car, I would never have got dem keys. No, sah! " He shook his head vigorously. " Not in a hundred years would I hab got dose keys."

" It's a good thing you did, but where's the first garage? "

" Where dey hab de Buick? "

" That's right," said Martin patiently.

" Dixon's Garage, sah, on de Dorchester Road. It ain't so much ob a garage. Jest a one-eyed shack of a place, but dese days Massa Fane gets most of his petrol and spares from Dixon's."

" Do you know them well? "

" Why, sho' I do. Massa Dixon's a very nice gentleman, and——"

" Telephone him, Sampson. Tell him I'm calling soon and I want to hire that Buick, or some other fast car. I may need it for two or three days. Tell him to send the bill to my father, who'll take full responsibility."

Sampson said, " Where you going, Massa Martin? "

" To catch up with the others. And I'd like to borrow your bicycle."

" Why, sho', sho'," said Sampson. A grave expression filled his dark eyes, and his lips pressed together for a moment. " Yo' take my machine, Massa Martin, any place yo' like."

" You'll be able to pick it up at Dixon's Garage. And Sampson——"

" Yes, sah? "

" I expect Mr. Medley will be here again soon, and he'll want to know where we've gone. You don't know, so you can't tell him. You aren't to tell him anything about me going to Dixon's Garage. You aren't to say a word."

" Not one word," said Sampson, shaking his head. His eyes seemed to become more prominent, he moved his hand forward and touched Martin's arm lightly. " Massa Martin, sah."

" Yes, old chap? "

" Yo' in mighty serious trouble, ain't you? "

" Yes, Sampson, but not the way you think."

" I doan' know so much," said Sampson. " I'm terrible worried 'bout you and Massa Richard. Terrible worried. Massa Martin, I'm just a house-boy, I ain't no right to say anything 'bout what I'm going to say, but yo'll forgive me, sah. If yo' in trouble, tell yo' pa. Don't keep anything from him, Massa Martin."

" I won't, Sampson! "

Martin gripped his hand, then turned abruptly, and pushed the bicycle out of the garage. As he stepped into the sunlight and looked down the drive, he saw a car turn in at the gates. Medley's. He went quickly by the side of the garage.

" Remember, you don't know a thing, Sampson."

" No, sah! "

Martin pushed the bicycle along the paths of the vegetable-garden, deserted just then, and towards a gate which led to a copse, near the house. The sun was shining on the bright, fresh green of beech and birch, and on an occasional oak. Crows were flying about the tops of the trees, cawing occasionally; a robin flitted across his path; he heard a rustle of dry leaves and young under-growth as a rabbit scuttled to its burrow. There was a path here which led to the village; it was a handy short cut, they'd often used it when boys. He mounted the machine and, hidden from the house and grounds by the trees, pedalled over the bumpy path, dodging roots of trees where he could, going into holes he couldn't avoid. The ride took him nearly ten minutes. He didn't go into the village, but across a field behind it, and struck the main Dorchester road a few hundred yards from the village itself. Two or three people were in the back gardens of a row of cottages near the grey stone church; he saw no one he recognised.

The garage, just a tumbledown shed with a few tyre and oil signs, lay back from the road. Two dilapidated cars were standing outside it, with *For Sale* tickets on them, and beyond them a huge black Buick limousine; it looked newer than the Blond Beauty.

As Martin put the cycle against the wall a middle-aged man in his shirt-sleeves came out, wiping his dirty hands on an oily rag. He had a fringe of grey hair and a bald patch, his face was as brown and weathered as a piece of old teak, his body was like a barrel, and he moved with a sailor's roll.

" Afternoon, sir! " His voice was breezy. " What can I do for you? "

" I'm Martin Fane. I think Sampson——"

" Well, fancy me not recognising you! " boomed Dixon with a voice that must have been trained to sound through miles of fog. " Split image you are, Mr. Martin, a younger edition of the old man himself! Want to use the Buick, Sampson tells me. Help yourself. Anything I can do for the son of Jonathan Fane, and it's as good as done."

" Is that one ready for the road? " Martin nodded towards the Buick.

" Had her out myself this morning, showing a client," said Dixon. " Price is right, but she uses a lot of petrol, it wouldn't be honest if I didn't admit that. Still, she does seventeen miles to the gallon on a long run, and you can't really complain! "

" Petrol in now? "

" Tank's filled up—I did that the minute Sampson 'phoned me. You can do two hundred miles on her, without a stop! That's if you want to. How's Mr. Fane to-day? Writing one of his bloods? I don't mind admitting," went on Dixon earnestly, " I don't know how he does it. Takes me all my time to write a letter. I wouldn't have his job if you paid me a thousand a year."

He beamed, and showed several gold-capped teeth, as they went to the car. Martin took the wheel.

"What's the matter with your arm?" asked Dixon quickly. " Look's a bit awkward."

"Just a scratch."

"Now be careful, Mr. Fane, don't go taking any chances."

Martin chuckled.

" I won't! "

He started the engine, let in the clutch, and eased the car towards the road. A tradesman's van passed. He looked towards the village, wondering if Medley would come back quickly; wondering, also, if Medley had telephoned an emergency call to Dorchester; he might think it worth holding any member of the Fane family seen on the road. Nothing was in sight.

" All clear, off you go, sir," said Dixon breezily. " If you find you like her, you could have her for three-fifty. Don't forget! " He beamed and saluted. " It's a bargain."

Martin swung on to the road.

.   .   .   .   .

Morden Street, Chelsea, was near the river, a street of large houses, a few of them standing in their own grounds, most in narrow terraces. It was a quiet district. A few plane-trees grew at intervals along the street, and there were ornamental trees in most of the gardens. As Martin drove along it, looking for Number 31, a police-man on a bicycle turned a corner and came towards him. Martin felt his nerves grow tense, but the man only glanced incuriously, more at the car than at the driver, and passed by.

Number 31 was near a corner, one of the houses standing in its own grounds. The grounds here seemed to be well-kept, although gloomy in the evening light. There was a beech-hedge behind a low brick wall, which seemed to run right round the garden. One side was overgrown, with shrubs and bushes making a thick cover for the front door when one approached from the gates; these were closed.

Martin drove a little way past, and pulled up round a corner. He got out, walked back, and strolled casually towards the gates. No one was about, and everything was quiet.

He felt the gun in his pocket, and made a sudden decision. He opened the double gate, pushed it back, and walked briskly towards the front door. There was a small, square porch, made of red brick like the walls, and the front door was painted green. The brasses at the knocker and letter-box needed polishing. It was probably a silly thought, but the house had a deserted look; as if it were empty.

Little pieces of gravel from the drive covered the floor of the porch, and they looked fresh; so someone had been here lately. He was studying them more closely when he saw something different—a large, reddish spot. He stared at it tensely; there were others, smaller, which led towards the door and disappeared beneath it; they showed up a brownish red on the grey stone of the doorstep. He bent down and examined them more closely. Blood?

He took out his penknife and broke the browny red film; beneath, it was crimson. This was blood. His heart began to hammer as he straightened up. There was no blood on the drive. As far as he could see, it started just inside the porch; and whoever had been injured had gone inside. He tried the door; it was locked.

He swung round, hurried towards the side of the house, and then towards the back; his mind full of urgent questions, and a picture of Barbara in his mind's eye.

179

The back door was also closed, and when he pushed it he thought that it was bolted. A tall, narrow window was at one side, and the garden here was protected by shrubs and trees.

He picked up a small stone, which made a border to a flower-bed, and hurled it at the window. The crash of breaking glass seemed loud enough to disturb the whole neighbourhood. He backed towards the shrubs and stood where he couldn't be seen from the house or from gardens nearby, and listened intently.

He heard no other sound.

After at least two minutes he stepped forward. No one had appeared at any of the windows in sight. He had made a big hole in the glass, near the door, and put his right arm through it, and groped for the key. He couldn't see. He scratched his wrist slightly, winced, and went on groping, and touched the key.

He grunted as he exerted himself to turn it; the strain on his fingers was excruciating, but suddenly he heard the lock click back. He withdrew his arm cautiously, then tried the door. It opened.

He stepped into a gloomy scullery, closed the door behind him, and stood in silence. There was no sound. He moved past a big, old-fashioned gas-stove towards a door which stood ajar, stepped through this doorway into a kitchen, and then heard a sound which made him start.

It was a clock, striking.

He gulped, and stood quite still, counting the booming notes. Seven. He glanced at his watch, it was certainly much later than that, he hadn't left the garage until half-past five.

It was nine o'clock. He'd probably lost two strikes while his heart had palpitated so much. He went on, more quickly, the gun held tightly inside his pocket. The next room was a big, comfortable-looking kitchen; beyond that was a passage, and in the hall at the end of it stood a grandfather clock in a carved oak case. He went towards it, seeing that the hands pointed to nine; if he couldn't control himself better than he had so far, he might as well have stayed away.

The hall, large and square with a few pieces of old-fashioned furniture in it, had a fitted carpet; there was no one in it, and there was no sound anywhere in the house. He went to the front door. The hall was gloomy, for dusk would soon fall, and the only light came through coloured-glass windows on either side of the front door and from a narrow fanlight above it.

The spots of blood were there, and they led across the carpet towards a room on the left of Martin. The door was ajar. He went towards it cautiously. If he'd ever doubted that this wasn't the kind of job he wanted, he knew now.

He pushed the door wider open.

The blinds were down, and there was little light; big furniture showed against the walls, and the carpet muffled the sound of his footsteps. He groped for the electric light switch, found three, and pressed one down.

Richard sat in an easy-chair, hands tied to the arms, legs tied to the feet, and something tied round his mouth. His eyes were glittering and darting to and fro.

Jonathan Fane was lying on the floor near the chair, tied hand and foot. There was a cut on the back of his left hand, which had obviously bled freely. A scarf was tied round his face, too, and his eyes were wide open. By his foot lay a newspaper, smeared with blood, and by that was a cream-coloured envelope.

" I've been glad to see you before," said Richard with difficulty, " but never as glad as this. In future, whatever you say about anything goes with me, and if the Maestro starts to argue I'll deal with him."

He smiled painfully. There were ridges at the side of his mouth, where the scarf had bitten into the flesh, and it looked red and sore. His voice was hoarse. He was sitting in the chair, rubbing his wrists gently; ridges, where the cord had bitten, showed up clearly on them. He didn't say so, but pins and needles were making agony in his arms and legs.

Martin stood in front of his father, who was now sitting in another easy-chair, free of his bonds. Martin had fetched a towel and a bowl of water from the kitchen, and was bathing the cut. It looked worse than it was; it certainly wasn't so bad as Martin's bullet wound. Fane didn't speak or wince while Martin worked, but his eyes were bloodshot, and there was a bruise on the side of his chin. Richard appeared to be unhurt.

" That'll do, Scoop," Fane said.

" I'll get something to bandage that with, now."

" We've too much to do to worry about that."

Fane was very husky.

" We haven't," said Martin, and smiled grimly.

" You know now what it's like to have a son who takes after you in all respects, including stubbornness," said Richard. " Could I do with a drink! "

" The kettle's on," Martin said. " I can't find whisky or anything potent."

Richard gulped.

" You mean—*tea*."

" Yes. I'll be back in a couple of minutes."

Martin turned out of the room, knowing that the others were staring at each other, astounded at his calmness. He forced himself to move slowly, and not to let his feelings run away with him; panic or careless haste wouldn't help. The others were at the end of their tether. They hadn't had lunch; that meant they hadn't eaten since breakfast. He'd had a later breakfast and yet felt fiercely hungry.

The house was obviously lived in, and he found bread and butter and some cheese in a big larder. He cut off hunks of bread, buttered it liberally, put it on a tray with the cheese and several plates, and then made the tea. Next, he rummaged through some drawers, found a clean white tablecloth, made several cuts at one edge and then tore it into strips. He put these on the tray, and went back into the front room.

It was about twenty minutes since he had found the others. The newspaper and the cream-coloured envelope were still on the floor. Until Richard had started to speak, neither of them had said a word, their mouths had been too stiff. He put the tray down on a large round table in the middle of the room.

" Man of miracles," said Richard.

" Martin, have you telephoned the police? " asked Fane.

" Not yet, Dad."

" You should, right away. It was folly to try to do anything ourselves."

" Have a drink first and talk afterwards," said Martin carefully.

He poured out, putting plenty of milk and sugar into the cups; none of them took sugar, but they needed something as a stimulant, and he hadn't found any spirits. He took them their cups; his father had difficulty in shifting his, Richard was in slightly better shape.

Martin drank his tea, then picked up the newspaper and the envelope. It was sealed and familiar-looking. He didn't have to ask where he had seen one like it before; Gillian Dunn had shown him four of the same manufacture, all addressed to Raymond.

From the front page of the *Evening Echo* photographs of his mother and father stared up at him; and both were good likenesses. He clenched his hands at sight of his mother; she looked younger there. She had often complained that she didn't photograph well, but this one couldn't have been bettered.

The headline ran: " AUTHOR'S WIFE KIDNAPPED."

" Mrs. Evelyn Fane, wife of Jonathan Fane, world-famous writer of crime stories, was kidnapped to-day from the sleepy Dorset village of Lichen Abbas. The *Echo* understands——"

He didn't want to read what the *Echo* understood. He glanced at the stop press, and saw:

" Lionel Robertson, private inquiry agent of 227a Strand, found shot in his office late this afternoon. Death was instantaneous. Superintendent Bellew of Scotland Yard in charge."

Martin looked up.

" How did you get here? " Jonathan Fane asked.

" Let's leave that, shall we? " Martin looked hard at the envelope, which was addressed to Jonathan Fane. The writing was unfamiliar. " How did you run into this packet? "

" We found one of the blackmailing letters at Nye Street," said Fane.

" I thought you'd searched the place," said Richard, trying to be bright. His eyes were glittering, he was talking to hide his strong emotions—he always talked too freely when he was strung up to a high pitch of nervous tension. " The Maestro did the obvious thing, went straight to Raymond's clothes, in the wardrobe. A letter was in the pocket—and told Raymond to come here, as

184

usual. We came. We just rang the bell, and your friend Garrett opened the door. He had a knife, and the Maestro had a crack at him. You can see the result. Several of them were here. We were both bumped on the head, and I thought the end had come."

Martin didn't speak.

"We had a narrow squeak at Guildford, too," said Richard. "As we left a police car turned the corner. They'd taken their time, hadn't they? I don't know whether they'd been at Nye Street before, but it was empty when we got there. You'll be interested to know that the Maestro can force a Yale lock with ridiculous ease, he must have taken lessons off old lags."

"Wasn't it pretty crazy just to walk up to the front door?" asked Martin.

Fane said, "Yes, of course it was. On the other hand, these people didn't kidnap your mother because they've any spite towards her. They wanted to be able to dictate terms. I thought that they would be prepared to parley."

"And the villain didn't turn out according to the text-book. It was probably not the right villain."

Richard actually grinned. Martin nodded; he could understand it, and understand, too, that although his father hadn't said so in so many words, he would have been prepared to negotiate with Smart Rummy for his wife's safety. Any one of them would have done that.

"How did *you* find the address?" Fane asked.

Martin said slowly, "Barbara telephoned me. She gave this address, said she was coming here." The words were received in silence, and he went on quickly, "There's been some more nasty business at home. Gillian Dunn died this morning. Morphine poisoning, and I gathered from Tucker that she must have taken the stuff some time to-day. I was waiting for Medley when Barbara telephoned. Then Smart Rummy called me up, and told me to do nothing with the diamonds yet. If I had the damned things, I would have told him I'd do a deal right away. As I hadn't, I thought desperate measures were called for, and took a chance with Barbara. As well I did."

The others nodded.

" What's the *billet doux*? " Richard asked. " Oh, that reminds me. Have you read the stop press? "

" Robertson was on the 'phone to me when it happened. He wanted to know if I knew where Barbara was. I decided that if someone thought it worth killing him, he was certainly not on the side of the crooks, and that probably meant that Barbara wasn't, either."

" I doubt if she is," said Fane quietly.

Without another word Martin tore open the letter. It was written in pencil, in block capitals. It was even and regular, and the wording showed that it was written by someone reasonably well educated. He read it aloud, very softly :

> " My dear Jonathan Fane,
>
> " Isn't it time you stopped pretending that you and your bright sons have stepped out of the pages of one of your books? This is serious. You will not see your wife again unless the diamonds are made available. I will send a messenger shortly to read you this note. You will tell the messenger where the diamonds are hidden. If your information is accurate you will later be released. So will Mrs. Fane. Otherwise you will not see your wife alive again."

.   .   .   .   .

Richard got up slowly, held on to the arms of his chair for a few moments, and then began to hobble round the room. He kept wincing. His father started to get up, and Martin helped the older man, whose legs nearly gave way under him, but he wouldn't sit down again. Martin let him lean heavily, and they walked round half a dozen times, until Richard was able to move fairly freely and Jonathan Fane had reasonable control of his legs.

Richard lit a cigarette from the stub of another.

"Well, what?" he asked in a strangled voice. "We're now clueless. Unless we go to the police I don't think we have a chance, and if we go to them, Smart Rummy might prove to be a man of his word." He caught his breath. "This is hell!"

"Did you go to Percy Mellor's garage?" Martin asked.

"No, we cut it out. I can't believe that Mellor——"

"We may have to believe that Mellor's mixed up in it!" cried Martin. "If Raymond's body was in that car when we took delivery, then——"

"The man wouldn't be crazy enough to do it!"

"I don't think it was crazy."

"It would force the police to question him."

"And he'd make out a good case for himself," Martin said. "It might be possible to scare him and make him talk."

"I don't think he knows anything." Richard was pacing up and down now. "Oh, he may, of course. He's worth trying. Anything's worth trying. I can't stop here and do nothing. Damn it, *could* they commit murder in cold blood? If Mother——"

"They've committed three," Jonathan Fane reminded him quietly. "They'll be prepared to commit a fourth. Judging from what we know of the man Rummy, he won't waste a lot of time." He pushed his fingers through his grey hair, and looked much older than when they'd reached Nairn Lodge; and much more grim, and he spoke with great emphasis. "We must wait until we hear from Rummy again. We must not tell the police, at this stage. As far as I can see, whatever we tell the police will be suspect. Medley wasn't convinced that you were quite innocent. I don't blame him. When we've heard from Rummy we may come to terms. I've enough money to pay——"

He broke off. His eyes glowed, unexpectedly, as if new hope had been poured into him. The others stared as he moved to the table and snatched up the letter, and read:

187

" ' I will send a messenger shortly to read you this note.'
We're slow! Do you realise what that means? He's
going to send someone here, someone who will assume
that we're still captive."

After a tense silence Richard breathed, " Good Lord,
yes! "

" I don't get it," said Martin slowly. " If he's going to
send someone, why did he leave the note behind in the
first place? It doesn't add up."

" It's what he says," Jonathan Fane declared, " and we
can expect a visitor. I——"

" Listen! " exclaimed Richard.

The others turned towards the window. Martin
moved suddenly, reached the door, and switched off the
light; darkness fell upon the room like a blanket. Outside, they heard the engine of a car; heard the car change
gear. It drew nearer; there was no doubt that it was
coming near.

" Well, well! " breathed Richard. " We're going to
have a chance of knocking the stuffing out of one of them.
If we can't make him talk, between us, we'll deserve all
we'll get."

" He'll talk," said Jonathan Fane in a low-pitched
voice; it would not have done the caller good to hear him.

He moved a little nearer the window, as headlights
turned towards them, shone eerily through the slats of the
Venetian blinds, and were then switched off. The car
stopped. The men could not see one another, could only
hear each other breathing.

Richard whispered, " Behind the door, Martin. He'll
come straight in here."

Martin said, " All right."

He moved towards the door, knocked against the table,
heard Richard say " *Quiet!* " and, with his hand outstretched, touched the wall. He was near the door and
the light switches. He heard a key turn in the lock of
the front door; the door of this room was open a few
inches, just as it had been when he had arrived. He

stared at it. Light shone in suddenly, as a switch was pressed down in the hall.

He knew who it was; had been afraid of it when he had heard the high-powered engine of the car. These were the footsteps of a woman.

She drew nearer and pushed open the door. Her shadow appeared on the floor, and grew longer as she stepped inside, groped for the light switch, and pressed it down.

Martin stepped forward swiftly, banged the door to, and gripped her arm.

" Hallo, Barbara," he said softly.

SHE caught her breath; it was almost a scream. Martin's grip on her arm tightened. In spite of the circumstances he remembered when he had last held her tightly; in his room, when he had been convinced that everything about her was good. Now he stared at her, his face set and savage anger in his eyes. She glanced at him, then at his father and Richard. She didn't try to pull herself free, but stood absolutely still.

" You—came," she breathed.

" Oh, yes," said Martin. " I'm fool enough for anything; almost."

She pulled her arm free, and he didn't stop her. He stepped to the door, so that it wouldn't be possible for her to make a sudden rush and get out. His fingers closed about the gun in his pocket. She took a few slow steps towards Jonathan Fane, and the glitter in his eyes must have told her what he thought.

" Little Delilah," Richard said softly. " How I'd love to see you hang! "

" Where is my wife? " Fane asked.

His voice was low-pitched, but quivered a little. That was all he wanted to know, the only concern he had.

Barbara said, " I don't know."

" So little Delilah doesn't know," said Richard softly. He drew nearer her, and took her wrist. " Little Delilah is going to think again, or else she is going to get hurt. She's going to tell us where to find Mother, and how we can get her. She is also going to tell us the name of her boss, her real boss, this time. After that, she is going to have some friendly interviews with the police. If she doesn't start thinking those second thoughts soon, she's

going to get *badly* hurt. Martin is the quixotic member
of this family." He paused, raised her arm as if he would
twist it, and snapped viciously, " Where's my mother? "

" Let her go, Richard," Fane said.

" Like hell I will! Look what she's done to Martin.
Look what she's done to Raymond and to Gillian.
Remember? Gillian died from poisoning administered
at home, *Barbara* had a good chance to give her that.
Didn't you, Delilah? Where is my mother? "

" I don't know," Barbara said, and the words seemed
to be forced from her lips. The light, softened by
alabaster shades, made her look very pale. She hadn't
made up lately, her lipstick had smudged at one corner,
and her eyes were feverishly bright. " If I knew, I'd
tell you."

" You'll tell——" began Richard.

" Let her go, Skip." Jonathan Fane's voice was sharp.
" At once."

Reluctantly Richard released her arm. She lowered it
to her side, put her other hand to her forehead, and turned
to look at Martin. He hadn't moved from the door.

" You needn't swoon," Richard sneered. " We're not
soft-hearted. At least, *I'm* not soft-hearted."

" Did Rummy send you? " Fane asked.

" Yes," said Barbara.

Until that moment, Martin had hoped that there might
be an explanation which would clear her of suspicion;
the admission damned all chance of it. He kept quite
still, feeling as if he were burning with hatred. Richard
swung on his heel, snatched out his cigarettes, and lit one.
He flicked the match across the room; it struck against
some fire-irons and dropped; it hadn't gone out, and
burned brightly on the tiled hearth.

" What were your instructions? " Fane asked.

He kept his head much better than Martin could have,
or Richard; but it was obvious that he was holding his
feelings in check. Martin thought that it would take very
little to make him burst the bonds of his restraint.

" I was to come here, remove your gags, and read to you a note that was left on the floor," she said. " Then I was to try to persuade you to tell me where the diamonds are hidden."

Barbara spoke in a flat, monotonous voice, and each word seemed to be an effort. She looked from one to the other; if there was anything stranger, it was the fact that she didn't refuse to meet their eyes.

" Were you here before? " asked Fane.

" Yes."

She turned quickly towards Martin, looked as if she were going to say more, and then changed her mind. She backed a pace and opened her hand-bag. Quick as a flash, Richard strode across and snatched it out of her hand. He took it to a table and turned it upside down. Everything that Martin had seen in the bag fell out— including the diagrams of the diamonds.

" I was going to light a cigarette," she said.

" That can wait. I was making sure you didn't pull a gun, Delilah."

" Give her a cigarette, Skip," said Fane.

" Damn it, no! She——"

" Don't be difficult," said Fane. " We're civilised, even if Rummy isn't." The edge was still on his voice, but he had lost something of the tension. " So Smart Rummy still thinks we have the diamonds? "

" He says that he knows Martin has them."

The words seemed to hurt as she uttered them. Richard had shaken some cigarettes forward in his packet, and held it out to her. Now he snatched it back, but she hardly noticed them. She brushed the hair back from her forehead again; her eyes were so bright against her pallor that they looked unnatural.

" That old canard," Richard growled. " It——"

" Be quiet, Skip," said Fane patiently. " Martin, I can't believe that you would hold these diamonds, knowing what's happened. Your mother's life is at stake; you realise that, don't you? "

" The only diamonds I've ever had are those I left at the bank. You said they were fakes."

Barbara exclaimed, " What? "

" That's right, fakes," jeered Richard. " Perhaps you're beginning to realise that you and your friend Rummy aren't so clever. Martin forced open that deed-box, found some sparklers, and took them to his bank. That's what an honest man does. They were paste, according to Father."

" According to the police," corrected Fane.

Barbara backed towards a chair, and dropped into it. That news was obviously out of the blue, and shocked her; she was quivering. She looked round at Martin, who hadn't stirred from his position, and her voice was unsteady.

" Martin, can you prove that? "

" It's what happened."

" The diamonds in the deed-box were *false*? "

" Which means that Raymond Dunn didn't have the real ones," said Richard.

" Oh, no, it doesn't," said Barbara quickly. She stood up again and fiddled with some ornaments on the mantel-piece. " Raymond had the real diamonds, there's no doubt about that. He acted as intermediary between a number of jewel-thieves and Smart Rummy. Rummy always kept in the background, as I told you, it isn't until this case that he seems to have shown himself at all—on the road, when you were held up. And that might not have been Rummy. I——"

" Don't you know who he is? " Fane asked sharply.

She hesitated.

" Why ask her anything? She'll only lie," said Richard.

" I don't know who Rummy is, I'd never spoken to him until to-day," she said. " We talked in this house. I was blindfolded and didn't see him. I heard only so much. I believe that he'll carry out his threat unless he gets those diamonds. He walked into Robertson's office this afternoon, because Robertson had discovered who he was. He shot Robertson in cold blood. He'll shoot anyone to get what he wants."

"Who is he?" Fane asked abruptly.

"I tell you I don't know," Barbara insisted. "He told me that Robertson had found out, and I've read about what happened. The thing that matters is to convince him that you haven't the diamonds."

"Tell us who Rummy is!" barked Richard.

Jonathan Fane said, "Be quiet a minute, Skip." His calmness was almost unnatural. "Barbara, you were telling us that you were quite sure that Raymond Dunn had the real diamonds."

"Oh, yes. They were given to him by the thief. He welshed—paid a little on account, but not the balance of the money. Rummy had already paid him the full price to pass over to the thief. Instead of being satisfied with his commission, Raymond held most of the money and the diamonds themselves."

"How do you know all this?"

Barbara said, "Robertson discovered who had stolen them in the first place, and talked to the thief early this morning. He telephoned from your house. That's why we left. I went to see Robertson after I'd talked with you, Martin, and convinced him that you hadn't got them. He decided to have a crack at the thief. There isn't any doubt that Raymond Dunn had them. The pitiable fool! He should have known that Rummy would never let him get away with them. Raymond discovered that it was Rummy who was blackmailing him, and he tried to get his own back. He was running away from Rummy, who caught up with him. Rummy killed him."

"How do you know it was Rummy?" asked Fane softly.

"Rummy told me so himself." Barbara sounded very tired. "He wasn't boasting—it was just to make sure that I realised that he meant what he said. He also said that he was keeping Pete Dunn prisoner. Pete found out too much. I imagine Raymond told him something. It's—dreadful. They tortured Raymond before he died, and he broke down and told them where the diamonds were—in the deed-box under the floor in his bedroom. Garrett saw the box, and then Martin attacked Garrett. That's why Rummy was so sure that you had them. So— Raymond lied."

She leaned back with her hands on the arms of her chair, and her fists were clenched.

" Or could you be lying? " sneered Richard.

" No," she said wearily, " I'm not lying. You won't believe me, but I work for the Relvon Insurance Company, and I've been trying to find out who Rummy is, and whether he had a cache of stolen jewels. I think he has. He took chances, because of the trouble with the Rossmore stones, otherwise I doubt if he would have been in difficulty now. He's been so used to getting exactly what he wants and feeling quite secure that he's come to think he's unbeatable. He's completely without feeling, he's just—bad." She shivered. " I'd known for some time that Raymond Dunn was a go-between—handling stolen jewels and passing them on to the buyers, that's why I got in touch with his brother. And because Pete Dunn ran into trouble——"

She held her breath, as if it hurt her to go on.

" Yes," said Jonathan Fane, and his voice was surprisingly gentle.

" I was going to say, that's what brought your sons into it," said Barbara. " You couldn't have had worse luck. Rummy is absolutely ruthless. You can't reason with him, he's so sure that nothing will go wrong. The only possible chance of saving Mrs. Fane is to get the diamonds for him, and——"

She broke off again.

" If you tell us who he is we can inform the police," said Fane, and he sounded absurdly formal. He changed his tone abruptly. " How did you happen to come here and fall into the hands of Smart Rummy? "

Barbara said, " Robertson told me about this house, it was almost the last thing he said to me. He didn't want me to come, said it might be dangerous. I didn't tell him I was coming. The only person I told was Martin, on the phone——" She broke off, then went on quickly, " I got in, listened to what the men were saying, heard what Rummy was planning, then I was caught. I was blindfolded before I was taken in to see Rummy. He told me simply and cruelly that unless I did exactly what I told him he would kill Mrs. Fane. He also said that if the police discovered who he was, she would be killed. That's why I'm here now. He took me away and then sent me back as soon as he and his gang had cleared out and covered their tracks. He sent a man with me. He's outside now. You're to tell me where to get the diamonds, and I'm to tell his man outside. The rest you know."

" I don't believe it," said Martin flatly.

It was so long since Martin had spoken that Barbara started, and turned her head quickly. He moved forward for the first time since she had come into the room. She didn't cringe back when he reached the side of her chair and stared down. He put his right hand under her chin and forced her head up, so that if she had had her eyes open she would have to look into his face.

"You're lying," he said.

"It's the truth, Martin."

"Who is Rummy?"

"I don't know. If I did, and told you, your mother would die. I wouldn't dare do it."

"My mother means nothing to you. If you were able to tell the police it would be a personal triumph, and if you're really working for Relvon it would make you for life. You're lying."

Her eyes pleaded with him.

"It's the truth. I've told you everything, I couldn't name him to save my own life. You must understand the situation. I have, from the beginning. I've never doubted Rummy's devilishness. I'm scared, but I'm quite sure that he will do what he says. I'll try to convince him that you haven't the diamonds. I don't think he'll believe it."

"I'll make him believe it," Martin said. "I'll see him myself. Where is he?"

She didn't answer.

"She's incapable of telling the truth," said Richard thinly. "She knows, all right."

Fane came across, and they were all three close together. Martin took his hand away from Barbara's chin, but kept looking at her, as if willing her to talk.

" Don't do anything foolish, Martin. There's a man watching outside. I must have been here nearly an hour —he was told to come and see what was happening if I stayed over an hour. I was allowed that time to persuade your father and Richard to tell me where to find the diamonds. I'm due to leave at any time, now. Don't do anything foolish, let me try to convince Rummy." When none of them spoke, she went on, " It would help if I had the paste gems, to show him. When he knows he'll go into a rage, he might do anything, he—he just isn't normal. I heard him this afternoon, one of the men did something he didn't like."

She got up slowly.

" Where's this man? " Martin asked abruptly.

" In the street, but——"

" We might as well bring him in to join the party."

Richard swung towards the door.

" Don't go! " Barbara cried. " He's armed! "

" We're not so scared of our skins as you seem to be of yours," said Richard. " Right, Dad! Shall I go and collect him? "

Fane didn't answer at once, but looked intently at the girl. He was the only one who had not raised his voice against her, who had not tried to frighten her into talking. He backed away, and shook his head slowly.

" Look here—— " began Richard.

" Steady a minute," said Fane. " Are you sure he's in the street, Barbara, and not in another house? "

" Yes. It's a man Martin knows. Garrett. That's why Rummy sent him. Since what happened at Nye Street, Garrett's ready to kill. He's the most dangerous of Rummy's men—he's a coward, but he's crafty, and he won't think twice about killing. Mr. Fane, I know it's hard to believe me, I know neither of the others do, but I've told you the simple truth. There's only one chance—

to convince Rummy that Martin doesn't know where the diamonds are."

" How many men did he have with him? "

" I saw three. There may have been others."

" Are you sure there's only one outside? "

" I brought him as far as the gate."

" Why did Rummy send you and not just one of his men? "

" He thought you would listen to me."

" Look here," said Richard in a thin, incredulous voice, " if you go on like this, I shall begin to think you believe her. She's Delilah, remember, and——"

" I don't think so," said Jonathan Fane, and smiled faintly. " I think I'll take her at her word."

" You must be mad! "

" Oh, possibly," said Fane. " Barbara isn't convinced that if we were to get at Rummy we could outwit him. She's probably right, too. On the other hand, we must try. I think you'd better leave the house, Martin, and walk towards the end of the street. You came by car, of course."

" It's round the corner."

" Turn the corner and go to the car. Garrett will follow you. Richard and I will follow him, and we shall be able to deal with him, I fancy. If we bring him in here he may talk freely. You'll be able to show how persuasive you can be, Richard."

Barbara said, " Don't do it, please don't do it. If you leave this house, Garrett will shoot you. Let—let me go. He'll come and talk to me, and you may be able to catch him off his guard."

" What a hope! " Richard was relentless. " You'd tell him exactly what to expect."

" It might be better if Barbara goes," said Fane reasoningly. He glanced at Martin and smiled; and there was much more in the smile than appeared on the surface. " Ready to take the chance, Scoop? One way or another, you'll be able to settle your doubts about Barbara."

Martin drew in his breath.

" All right," he said.

Richard threw up his hands, helplessly, but didn't say another word.

. . . . .

Martin and Richard went out by the back door. It was pitch dark; clouds obscured the stars, and unless some-one was very near they couldn't be seen. They crept towards the front of the house, then went on to the grass verge near the bushes. It was not so dark there, because of the street-lamps. A car passed along the street, its engine whining; silence fell as it faded. They stood close together, Martin with the gun in his pocket and his fingers clammy about it.

They saw the light go out in the front room.

Soon there was a faint sound, as if the front door were opening. They just picked out Barbara's figure as she closed the door and stepped from the porch. She walked briskly towards the gates, and passed within a few feet of them. As she turned from the gate towards the corner the waiting men heard a man's voice.

They crept towards the gate.

Walking away from them were Barbara and another man, and the man might be Garrett; he was the right build. He had a hand on the girl's arm, and was speaking in an undertone, but the sound not the words travelled back to them. Richard quickened his pace, keeping close against the wall; Martin walked softly on the kerb. The man appeared to notice nothing. He was still talking.

Richard leapt.

Martin followed as the man spun round, and Barbara backed away. There was sufficient light from a street-lamp to show Garrett's face—and to show his hand moving swiftly towards his pocket. He didn't touch his gun. Richard smashed a blow at his chin, knocking him towards Martin, who timed an uppercut to perfection. Garrett went out on his feet.

" Back to the house! " hissed Richard.

Martin bent down. With both arms he could have lifted the unconscious man easily; with one it was difficult. As he tried, a car turned into the far end of the street, with its headlights on. He felt Richard push him aside. Richard grabbed Garrett, hoisted him, and staggered with him towards the Buick, just round the corner. He stood with Garrett leaning against the Buick when the other car passed.

Martin said, " Nice work. Put him in the car and we'll drive up to the house. It'll be safer."

.   .   .   .   .

Richard emptied a jug of water over Garrett's face, and the little crook moved his head slightly and licked his lips. His eyes flickered. Barbara stood in a corner of the room as if she were afraid of what would follow from this. Fane, still calm, watched as Garrett's eyes opened, closed again, and opened wide. Martin stood against the mantelpiece, looking much less grim.

" Wakey-wakey," Richard said brightly. " Show a leg, sailor! " He clenched his fist and aimed a blow at Garrett, missing by inches. Garrett flinched, but didn't speak. Richard had become a different man since this turn of events, and still had a broad smile. " That's a hint of what you'll get if you're difficult, Garrett."

Fane said, " Leave it to me, Skip, will you? "

" For a start," said Richard. " I don't promise not to take over if you make the usual hash of it."

" Sit up," Fane said to Garrett.

The man obeyed. It wasn't easy for him, and his head was doubtless swimming. It moved from side to side, as if he had no control over it, and his eyes rolled. Fane gave him a few minutes to get more control of himself, then spoke in a casual, almost friendly voice.

" You won't want to make trouble for yourself, Garrett. We intend to find Mrs. Fane. To do that we have to find Rummy. Where is he? "

Garrett didn't answer.

"You'll have to tell us, sooner or later," Fane said. "We don't intend to send for the police at this stage. You might keep mum with them, and they'd have no way of forcing you to speak. We have."

"*Have* we!" Richard chimed in.

"So make it easy for yourself. Where shall we find Rummy?" Fane asked. "You needn't worry about what he'll do to you, when we've found him we'll make sure he can't do any harm to anyone."

Garrett said thinly, "I don't know, and if I did I wouldn't tell you. Think you can catch Rummy? You haven't a dog's chance! When he finds that skirt——" He glared at Barbara, who stood quite still.

Martin went to her side and slid an arm round her waist.

"*He* won't save you, and no one will save Mrs. Fane, either," Garrett said. "Unless you let me go, Rummy will make her realise what it's like to——"

Jonathan Fane didn't speak, but smashed a clenched fist into the man's face. Garrett rocked backwards. Fane struck at him again, wildly, his eyes were glittering and his lips curled back over his teeth. Martin jumped forward and grabbed his father and pulled him away. Fane didn't struggle, but breathed heavily; he seemed to be fighting for breath. Garrett gulped and slowly sat up, and Richard pulled his arm and jerked him out of the chair, so that he stood swaying in front of them.

"Well done, Maestro," Richard said softly. "I wondered what was going to snap your tension. Garrett, there are three of us, and we all feel about the same. I will gladly beat you to pulp if you try to hold out. Where can we find Rummy?"

Martin let his father go.

Garrett closed his eyes, and muttered:

"He'll murder me, it isn't safe, he——"

Richard grabbed his arm and twisted.

"Where shall we find Rummy?"

Garrett gasped, "Let me go, let me go!" He pulled weakly, looked as if he were going to lose consciousness,

licked his lips and then went on as if he were in agony,
" I can't stand it, I can't stand it.   You'll find him at——"

The crack of a shot broke across his words, and a hole
gaped in his forehead.   It came with a paralysing sudden-
ness; for a split second no one moved but could only stare
at the little hole and the trickle of red.   The shot seemed
to have come from nowhere; and actually it had come
from the door.   Suddenly, Martin cried out:

" Look out, Bar! "

He flung himself forward and grabbed her, and they
fell together.   He crashed on to his wounded arm, and it
was torture.   He struggled and squirmed so as to shield
the girl, and stared towards the door.

Another shot rang out, the bullet buried itself in the
floor near his head.   Richard leapt towards the door, and
Jonathan Fane dodged to one side.   A bullet ploughed
through Richard's coat, and the door slammed.   They
hadn't caught a glimpse of the man who had fired.

RICHARD was near the door and grabbed the handle almost as soon as it slammed. Jonathan Fane called to him, but he took no notice, pulled the door open, and stepped swiftly to one side. Another bullet spat out, and buried itself in the wall; it missed him by inches. The front door opened and slammed, as Martin picked himself up and went to the window. His arm was shrieking with pain, but he snatched at the blind cord.

" Light! " he called.

Richard switched off the light, and as they plunged into darkness Martin had the blinds up. The light from the street-lamp was just sufficient to show a running figure. Martin cracked his gun against the window, and glass splintered. Richard disappeared, and next moment light streamed from the hall, out of the front door. It shone on the man who had half-turned, near the gates; but he fired towards the hall.

Martin squeezed the trigger, and the next moment he thought he saw the man flinch, but couldn't be sure. Before he could fire again the man turned and ran towards the gate, so he wasn't badly hurt. Richard appeared, racing down the short drive.

" He'll get himself killed," Jonathan Fane said, with a catch in his breath. " Skip! " He bellowed the nickname. " Come back! "

Martin flung the window up; they waited for the sound of another shot, but it didn't come. The engine of a car started up and roared as the car disappeared. Another roar sounded, nearer the house.

" That's Richard," Barbara said. " My car! "

" *Skip !* " roared Jonathan Fane again.

He couldn't be heard above the snorting of the engine as Barbara's M.G. hurtled along the street. The headlights showed the shrubs, the paint, and the posts and the walls of the houses opposite. The car swung left, at wild speed; and now it was almost impossible to tell the sound of one engine from another.

Barbara said brokenly, " I knew it would happen, the man's a devil."

" He hasn't won yet."

Jonathan Fane swung round towards Garrett. The man lay back in his chair, and the trickle of blood, very tiny, had reached one eyebrow and was creeping along it in each direction. Fane reached him, turned his coat back, and took out his wallet. He opened it and shook out the contents. Among the oddments of papers were several cards: business or visiting-cards. He picked one up, as Martin joined him, and they read it together: "Mellor's Garage, Gilling Street, Paddington. Presented By: *B. J. Garrett.*"

The name was written in ordinary writing-ink; the rest was printed.

Martin said in a strangled voice, " Bar, telephone the police. Coming or staying here, Dad? "

" I'm coming," said Fane. " Is the Humber——"

" Not here, they must have taken it. But I've a car."

Barbara didn't say a word to try to stop them, but watched as they hurried out. Martin turned to glance at her from the door, and gave a tight-lipped smile. She raised her hands and let them fall again. The two men ran down the drive; two minutes later she heard the engine of the Buick whine as the car moved along the road.

It would take them a quarter of an hour to get to Paddington.

She went across to the telephone and lifted it and began to dial 999. There was no ringing sound. She glanced at the body of the dead thief, and dialled again; there was still no ringing sound. Only then did she pause with the earpiece close to her ear; she could hear nothing, the usual buzzing sound didn't come. She banged the cradle of the receiver up and down, but nothing happened.

The telephone had been cut.

She turned and ran out of the house, and as she reached the drive a man and a woman turned in. The man called out nervously: " What's the matter? Did we hear shooting? " Footsteps were coming along the pavement, too, and a man with a deeper voice called out: " Now, what's all this? "

He appeared at the gateway; a policeman, walking quickly. Barbara rushed to him, but she had lost five precious minutes, another five would pass before she could tell the policeman what had happened.

She was almost incoherent, then she controlled herself, paused, and began to speak more calmly. A crowd had gathered and gaped at her, and the man seemed incapable of understanding. In fact, it was less than five minutes before he was on the way to a telephone.

. . . . .

Jonathan Fane was at the wheel, Martin giving directions. They turned off the Edgware Road into Praed Street, which was brightly lighted. People passed along the pavements, casually, buses lumbered past them, coming from Paddington.

" Next on the left, I think," said Martin. " We'd better try it."

He had been to Mellor's garage only once.

As his father turned the wheel, he told himself for the hundredth time since he had left Chelsea that the police would surely have questioned Mellor, that they should be watching him; but there was no certainty. He scanned the narrow street into which they turned, looking for the garage sign; there was none.

" Try the next right," he said.

Fane swung the wheel, but there was no garage in that street, either.

" Next left," said Martin.

Fane switched on the headlights as they turned the
corner. People were streaming along the road, and
Fane had to jam on his brakes. A bell clanged. The
significance of that didn't occur to them at first. Fane
drove more slowly, seeing the crowd in front of him,
thicker even than it was here; he could only crawl along.
Martin's forehead was wet with sweat. Minutes might
count, he'd not only forgotten the street but they couldn't
go back or get on at any speed.

He smelt burning.

The ringing sound took on a deeper significance then;
that was a fire-engine, so there was a fire nearby, and the
crowd was flocking to it. They reached a corner. The
street on the right was cordoned off by half a dozen
policemen, but the crowd were pressing forward. Several
fire-engines were in the narrow street beyond, men were
running about, lurid figures, thrown up by the red glow oι
the fire which burned fiercely and gave off thick volumes
of smoke.

Fane stopped the car.

A man near them said clearly, " It'll go up in five
minutes, with all that petrol."

Jonathan Fane gasped, leaned back, glanced at Martin
and said:

" *Petrol.*"

Martin opened his window. The smell was over-
powering now, unmistakably that of burning oil. He
also knew the place that was on fire, but wouldn't believe
it. He called:

" Where's Mellor's garage? Any idea? "

Two or three people turned, and a wag said loudly:

" Looking for the hot spots, chum? "

" Don't joke about it, George," said a woman with him.
" That's Mellor's garage, mister, it's just about burnt
out."

. . . . .

Afterwards Martin vividly remembered the way in
which his father handled the situation. The police let

them pass, after a word. The Fire Brigade Chief spared time to take them to a man from the Divisional Police-station. Jonathan Fane explained briefly who he was and why he was here. The Divisional Inspector didn't beat about the bush.

" We've been looking for you and your sons, Mr. Fane, the Yard sent out a general call. I can see why you're worried. We don't know how many people were inside, so far we've taken a man's body out. I'm afraid we shan't get anyone or anything else out to-night."

The glow of the fire was hot on their faces, steam rose with the smoke as the jets of water poured on to the adjoining buildings, the inside of Mellor's garage was a red-hot furnace.

" I'd like to see the body," said Jonathan Fane. " Has it been identified? "

" No. He was overcome by the fumes, I think. We found him lying face downwards, his legs pointing to-wards the door. We were able to pull him out, but there isn't much to recognise. It won't be pleasant."

" Never mind," said Fane. " Can you stand it, Martin? "

Martin nodded. He couldn't have talked, then, for the life of him. His mother might be in that inferno; his father knew that; yet could talk with outward calm, showing little or nothing of his feelings.

" This way," said the Divisional man.

A small shed, not far along, had been taken over by the police. The body of the victim lay on a bench which had been cleared of tools. A policeman was on duty at the open door, and a small crowd pressed round, trying to get a glimpse inside. The policeman put on a light as the little group entered.

The head and shoulders of the corpse was covered with a blanket. The feet and legs were hardly touched by the flames, but there were scorch marks and big burns near the waist. One hand was badly burned, and showed below the blanket; the other, the left hand, had hardly been touched. Fane approached, but Martin stood still, staring at that left hand and a ring on the little finger.

"You can have a look at the head if you like, but it won't be any good," said the Divisional man. "Do the clothes help?"

Fane said softly, "Thank God, it isn't Richard."

"Your other son? Is he——"

"That's Peter Dunn," said Martin in a muffled voice. "That's his ring."

"Sure?" asked the detective sharply.

"Yes," said Martin. "I'm quite sure."

. . . . .

They spent twenty minutes at the scene of the fire and half an hour at Scotland Yard at the request of a Yard man who soon arrived. He asked few questions, took Jonathan Fane's statement, forebore to reprove the Fanes, and offered to have them driven home to the London flat.

"I'll drive myself, thanks," said Jonathan Fane.

They reached the flat near Covent Garden just after one o'clock. Martin unlocked the front door, and darkness met him. Jonathan Fane said: "Not here, then," and went across to an easy-chair and sat down heavily.

He hadn't once said that he had hoped desperately that by now Richard would have reached the flat.

Martin went across to a box of cigarettes—Richard's—and lit one for himself. His father took one, but didn't draw at it. Now that the need for action was past he had sagged badly. He looked haggard and despairing; and Martin felt both. He telephoned the *Echo*. Tom Rowbottom wasn't in, but there was a simple message, left in case Martin called. It said: "No news."

"Nothing could have happened to Richard," Martin said with an effort, when he'd rung off. "He's chasing round——"

His father just looked at him, and his voice faded out. Martin cleared his throat.

"Like a cup of tea?"

" I suppose so," said Jonathan Fane. " I——"

The telephone bell rang.

Martin swung round towards it, but his father was out of the chair and at the instrument before Martin reached it. He snatched off the receiver.

" Fane speaking."

He caught his breath, but the flare of hope died out of his eyes, and his body drooped.

" No, we're not sure, Barbara," he said evenly. " Eh? Well, yes, if you'd like to. We'll expect you, then." He put the receiver down slowly and drew his hand across his forehead. It was smeared with sooty dirt, smuts were in his hair and over his linen jacket. " She's heard about the fire. She's coming round."

Martin grunted. He went into the little kitchenette and put on the kettle, marvelling that he could have felt a momentary lightening of his spirits; yet he had. He wanted Barbara to come. All doubt about her integrity was gone. Because of the fierce storm of events he seemed to have known her for years; he was desperately anxious to see her again.

She arrived in a taxi twenty minutes later. Martin opened the door, and they gripped hands but didn't speak. She glanced across at Jonathan Fane as Martin went to the tea-tray on the table.

" Have a cup? "

" Please." She went across and took Jonathan Fane's uninjured hand. " I'm so desperately sorry."

" Yes," said Fane. " Yes, I know. Don't let any of us waste time on self-reproach. We all did what we thought was the best thing. You haven't heard anything of Richard, have you? "

Barbara said, " Not really."

Obviously she hated saying that.

Martin swung round.

" What do you mean? "

" My car's been found," said Barbara. " The police told me just before I telephoned you. It was stranded near Morden Street. It's impossible to guess what happened."

" Is it? " asked Fane in a harsh voice. " Or isn't it easy? Rummy had others waiting, and Richard ran into a trap. Evelyn—Richard."

He sighed the words, leaned back and closed his eyes.

Barbara went across to Martin. Words served no purpose. Sleep was impossible, the thought of settling down for the night didn't occur to him. He wandered restlessly about the flat, and Barbara, keeping still, sat and watched as he picked up photographs of his mother, Richard, and Pete Dunn, all of which were on top of a book-case. He seemed to study each one in turn, as if seeking something in their faces which he had never seen before.

The telephone bell rang again. This time Jonathan Fane made no attempt to get up, but watched Martin move across to the instrument. It might be news of any kind—Richard, the police, the Press. Martin felt hope rising, but fought against showing it, lifted the receiver and said flatly:

" Martin Fane speaking."

" I thought you would be there," said a man in a now familiar voice. " I hope you've burnt your fingers enough. If you want to see your mother and brother alive again, you will do exactly what I tell you."

Martin held his breath.

Barbara came towards him, and Jonathan Fane got up slowly and took two steps forward.

" Can you hear me? " Smart Rummy asked.

" Yes."

" I shall send you instructions at eleven o'clock in the morning. By then you will either have the Rossmore diamonds or twenty-five thousand pounds in one-pound notes. I don't mind which. Have them ready on time, Fane."

He rang off.

" So they're alive," Barbara whispered.

Martin nodded.

Jonathan Fane went back to his chair and lit a cigarette; some of his movements were remarkably like Richard's, and he was sitting in Richard's chair.

" We can't be sure," he said gruffly. " Rummy would want us to think so, in order to squeeze."

" What are you going to do? " asked Barbara.

" Pay! "

Barbara said, " The police——"

" I know all the arguments," said Fane heavily. " I also know you're right, Barbara, it's folly to go on trying to handle this by ourselves. On the other hand, we know that Rummy will carry out his threats. By telling the police this we might catch Rummy; we would almost certainly condemn my wife and Richard to death. That's the side I have to think of."

" Yes, of course," said Barbara.

" Can you get the money? " asked Martin abruptly.

" Yes."

" I wonder where those diamonds are," said Barbara. " I wonder where Raymond put them."

" It hardly matters," Jonathan Fane said.

" I suppose not." Barbara went across and sat on the arm of his chair. " Why don't you go to bed for a few hours, Mr. Fane? There's nothing else we can do. It'll be much better if you're feeling fresh in the morning. One of us will stay awake, so that we don't miss any telephone calls. Won't you go and rest? "

" I should, Dad," Martin said. " I know it's impossible to go to sleep, but if you took your things off and got into bed it would help a bit."

Fane said slowly, " I suppose you're right." He didn't move, but lit a cigarette.

It was half an hour before he actually got out of the chair and went into Martin's room. Martin stayed with him until he had washed and undressed, lent him a pair of pyjamas, and waited until, after a straight look at his son, Fane went down on his knees by the side of the bed.

. . . . .

" He's praying," Martin said to Barbara in a broken voice. " He's gone down on his knees every night since I can remember. He——"

" Darling, don't upset yourself," Barbara said softly. " Try to relax. If you lie down too——"

" Oh, it's impossible ! "

" Sit back in a chair, then."

He shrugged, but had a quick bath and did what she advised. The waiting seemed interminable, and his mind was a prey to all manner of fears. At heart he did not expect to see Richard or his mother again. He was sure that his father didn't. When he closed his eyes, pictures of one came first and then of the other. He knew that Barbara was sitting watching him, but didn't open his eyes. Hundreds of times his father had imagined situations like this; hundreds of times he had tried to show what people felt. He'd never really succeeded in any of the books Martin had read.

He heard a door open, then slam. He opened his eyes and started up. Barbara was turning round in her chair as Jonathan Fane, wearing the borrowed pyjamas and his hair standing on end, stormed into the room.

" Martin ! "

" What is it ? "

" Where does Pete Dunn live ? "

" *Pete ?* In Bingham Street, but——"

" I don't think he's dead," said Fane in a shrill voice. " I don't think you saw his body. I knew there was

213

something strange about it. Remember what the police told us? He was lying with his head in the fire and his feet towards the street. If he'd been running away from the fire, he'd have fallen in the other direction. If he'd been pitched into it, it would explain his position. He——"

"But he had that ring! I wouldn't make a mistake about that."

"I haven't finished yet. The face was destroyed completely, and recognition would be impossible. Unless there was reasonable doubt about his identity, the police wouldn't check far. There was no one else there, no one in danger, and everything was so conveniently worked out. Why did they make sure his face and hair were burnt out of all recognition? Why?"

Fane's eyes were blazing.

Martin said slowly, "Dad, don't build up some fine theory that will collapse. If they'd killed him and didn't want the body found, they'd pitch him into the fire. That's reasonable enough."

"It could be what happened. It's equally possible that the man was thrown into the fire that way to make us think that Pete Dunn was dead. Don't interrupt! Pete was the reason for involving you in this, wasn't he? Pete was supposed to have gone to the rescue of his brother at Guildford. By then Raymond was in trouble with Rummy. If Pete and Rummy are the same man——"

"It's impossible!"

"It isn't impossible," said Fane fiercely. "It would answer a lot of things. If Pete is Rummy, he would have realised that there was a risk of being found out once Raymond turned against him. Pete disappeared suddenly, we took it for granted it was because he was in danger after trying to help Raymond. Supposing Raymond had discovered the identity of his blackmailer— and knew the truth about Rummy? Rummy's identity has never been known, he's been a shadowy figure, obviously building everything on keeping his identity secret. Now if Raymond discovered it, the only way to silence him would be by killing him. Robertson discovered who he was, and Robertson was killed."

Fane paused, but only for breath.

" Look here——" began Martin.

Fane brushed the interruption aside.

" Rummy wouldn't let Barbara see him. That might have been because she could describe him to the police afterwards, but could also have been because she would have recognised him. If she did, she would have been no use as a messenger."

" He spoke to her."

" Anyone can assume another voice, with practice. There's another thing. There's no reasonable doubt now that Raymond's body was put into the car at Mellor's garage. Raymond was almost certainly killed there. Who introduced Richard to Mellor? "

" Oh, that was Tom," said Martin quickly.

" Tom? "

" Tom Rowbottom. He brought Gillian to Nairn Lodge." Martin shook his head. " You can't pin that on Pete." Then he frowned as another thought came to him. " But Richard told Pete about the car on the phone before we bought it," he said, almost to himself. " Yes, and he mentioned Mellor's garage in Paddington."

" You see? " Fane said triumphantly. " It all fits."

Martin said slowly, " I can't believe it. Pete——"

" Another thing! " said Barbara. " It would explain why Pete telephoned to tell Gillian to get out of Seventeen Nye Street. If he knew that Garrett was on the way he'd want the house empty."

" He knew all right." Fane was fully convinced by his own arguments. " Where can we find Pete? "

" His cottage? " suggested Martin. " The police will have gone to his town flat at once, but he'd probably be safe down there for another day or so." Then he looked less confident. "Tom checked down there, and left a man to keep watch," he said.

" The chap he employed might have been bribed,"
Fane suggested. " Where did Rummy's call come
from? "

Martin said, " It was a local call."

" Sure? "

" I don't think there's any doubt. The operator didn't
come on, I just lifted the receiver, and he spoke—as he
would if he'd dialled the number. If it was Rummy who
shot at us to-night, he'd certainly be in or near London
now."

" Or on the way to his cottage. He'd leave someone
else to collect the ransom from us in the morning, he's so
often worked through others. In any case, he'd have
time to get to the cottage, leave the others there, and
come back to London by eleven. What's the address of
that cottage? "

Martin had already got out his address-book.

" Sea Rose, Adcombe Bay, near Weymouth," he said.

" We *must* tell the police," Barbara interrupted.

" Oh, no, we mustn't," said Fane abruptly. " If
they're waiting at the cottage when he arrives, he's
capable of killing Evelyn and Richard and then killing
himself. He won't let himself be caught."

Barbara said quietly, " You're wrong about the police,
Mr. Fane. They're not fools, and they'd do everything
they could to help. You're letting your emotions run
away with you. You are, you know." She had always
talked to Fane as if they were old friends and she could
safely argue and be sure he would listen. Fane didn't
interrupt her now. " In any case, we can't be certain
that Pete would go to this cottage. He is supposed to
have died to-night. He wouldn't show up at the cottage
to-morrow morning, and certainly wouldn't leave his
prisoners there. He'd be afraid that the local police
would call, to look round. It's most unlikely that he's
there. If we tell the police, they'll have a much better
chance of finding out where else he might be."

Into a long pause Martin said, " She's right, Dad."

" She's not," said Jonathan Fane. " Your mother may be there, and I won't take any risk at all."

Both the others knew that it would be useless to argue with him. They left half an hour later, with Fane at the wheel.

. . . . .

The roads were practically empty, and the black Buick had a fine turn of speed. They took it in turns to drive, and the speedometer hovered a great deal between seventy and eighty. They did a hundred and thirty miles in a little less than three hours.

At Dorchester they turned off the main road between Dorchester and Weymouth. It was daylight then, and they asked a man driving a milk-van where to find Adcombe Bay; he knew it well, and told them that there was only one cottage there. It was reached through a wooded patch of hilly land, close to the rocky coast. The sun shone brightly, and the sky was clear except for a faint haze in the distance, promising heat later in the day.

Martin led the way through a copse, and the dead leaves of the previous autumn muffled their footsteps. The rugged ground rose steeply until they came to a clearing, where the cliffs lay beyond, dropping almost sheer into the sea. They could hear the soft lapping of the water against the rocks and the sand below.

A little to the left, the cottage stood in the sun, small, brick-built, ugly. A path led from it towards a gap in the cliffs, which doubtless went down to the bay. By the side of the cottage stood a powerful Austin, glistening and new.

Pete Dunn hadn't owned a car like that.

Tom Rowbottom had just such a car on trial, had brought Gillian Dunn to Nairn Lodge in it.

Martin said in a queer voice, " That's not Pete's, that's Tom Rowbottom's."

27

JONATHAN FANE put a hand on Martin's arm, while Barbara looked at him as if she couldn't believe her ears. Nothing stirred near the cottage, there was no sign of life.

" Keep your voice low," said Fane. " If he's as deadly as we think, we mustn't give him any warning. There's a clear patch right round the cottage, so we shan't be able to approach without being seen, unless he's asleep. I should say that——"

" Let me go," said Barbara. " I can knock, and he'll probably come and see who it is."

" Oh, no," said Martin. " The moment he saw you he'd know the game was up. He'll probably be edgy and have a gun in his hand. I'll go."

" We ought to have had the police," Barbara said.

" If he saw the police he'd know there wasn't a chance," Martin said. " Dad was right. If he sees me he'll think I've come to talk business—or at least be prepared to. My job. No, Maestro," he added, as he saw his father's lips open. " You stay and look after Barbara."

Fane nodded.

Barbara started to speak again but stopped herself. Martin put his right hand into his pocket, about the gun. There were three bullets left. He waited for a few seconds, measuring the distance between these trees and the cottage itself, and decided that it was best to approach the back door; there was a blank wall there, without a window, and there was less chance of being seen.

He stepped from his cover.

The sun struck warm as he left the trees. There was grass half-way from the copse to the walls, then gravel.

His footsteps sounded very loud on the gravel, and he quickened his pace. He reached the back door. It was small and the green paint was peeling in places. He heard no sound from inside the house. He raised his hand to touch the handle, and wondered if it were possible that he was wrong, whether this had been a wild-goose chase.

The door was locked.

He could knock, and wait for Rowbottom to come and answer—and take a chance that Rowbottom would be sure that this meant trouble. Or he could break the door down. It looked as if it would give way under a heavy onslaught. He tried it with his right shoulder; it gave a little at the top, which suggested that it wasn't bolted there.

He was conscious of the anxious gaze from among the trees.

He drew back, measured the distance, and then flung himself at the door, putting every ounce of his strength behind it. The door creaked and groaned, and something cracked loudly. He drew back and flung himself forward again. The door flew open, there was a crack like a shot. He staggered into a small kitchen. A door ahead was wide open, and led into another room. He saw a man's feet, waving wildly. He rushed to the other room, and saw Pete Dunn struggling to get up from a couch.

. . . . .

So it was Pete.

. . . . .

Pete had obviously been asleep. He was snatching at a gun on a chair by the side of the couch, but missed it. Martin shot him through the hand and through the leg, and he collapsed, groaning.

There was no sign of Tom Rowbottom, but plenty of evidence against him.

. . . . .

Evelyn Fane and Richard were upstairs, on twin beds

in a small bedroom, bound hand and foot, and in a drugged sleep.

. . . . .

At eleven o'clock Tom Rowbottom called at the Fane brothers' London flat. The police were watching, followed him from the flat, and he went, unsuspectingly, to a house in Fulham. Percy Mellor and several others of the gang were there, and the police arrested them all without any trouble.

. . . . .

Sampson carried a tray of drinks into the drawing-room, later that evening, beamed around at everyone, took the tray first to Evelyn Fane, who looked tired but otherwise her usual self, hesitated, and then took it to Barbara, and also gave her a beaming smile. Then he went round to the men, serving Richard last.

"Where's yours, Sampson?" asked Jonathan Fane.

"Mine, sah? I don't drink with all you ladies and gennelmen present, sah, I——"

"Pour yourself a drink," said Jonathan Fane, looking up from his tomato juice. "And you give us the toast, Sampson."

"Me, sah? I neber could t'ink of any toast, no, sir! I just couldn't t'ink ob such a thing!" Sampson went across to the cocktail cabinet, poured out a drink with trembling hands, hesitated, beamed nervously round, and said, "Here's to hoping no sich thing as this ever happens again, sah!"

They were chuckling as he hurried out of the room.

Fane, leaning well back in his chair, smiled across at his wife, who had her legs stretched out on a pouf. She smiled back at him, looking calm and contented. Richard sat on the arm of a chair, swinging his right leg. Barbara and Martin were together on the Knoll couch.

"Well, why aren't you writing, Maestro?" asked Richard. "You've spent most of the day with the police, so you ought to be bristling with ideas."

" I think I'll take up writing romances after this," said Jonathan Fane dryly. " I'll be able to tell Scoop and Barbara how to go on."

" We're just waiting to learn," said Martin.

" Anyhow, you scored a bull," Richard said. " I wouldn't have got to Pete Dunn if I'd lived to be a hundred." They had told him everything that had happened, and he kept breaking out excitedly. " I came out worst, I think, Scoop's the real tough guy of the family. When I chased after Pete, from Morden Street, I simply ran into the trap. Impetuous and lacking sense." Richard laughed. " Pete was there waiting for me, and when I saw him I just stuck my neck out. His pals finished me off with a good clout over the head."

" At least they didn't clout me," said Evelyn Fane. " They just threw a sack over my head. But I was terrified! Darling, I don't think I'll ever be able to read a Fane Mystery again."

" You'll get over it," said Fane comfortingly.

Barbara said slowly, " Does anything ever really disturb you, Mr. Fane? I mean, once you're over the crisis."

" Nothing," said Evelyn, with feeling. " He's the most infuriatingly placid man I know."

" I'll tell you something to make you change your mind, one day," said Richard meaningly. " Well, it's over, thanks be! Pete, Tom, the ring-leaders in the jewel-thief gang, Mellor in on the ground floor, the other crooks mostly expert cracksmen, Raymond Dunn just a contact man. Martin, can you imagine him turning on his own brother? "

Martin said, " Yes, I think so. Raymond was the family's darling, inherited a fortune, was forgiven everything. Pete was cold-shouldered by the family. No reason for love, there. But Pete overdid his hate. He used Raymond as a contact man, and blackmailed him as well. It was to pay the blackmail that Raymond cheated over the diamonds—and that was Pete's undoing."

"One thing hasn't sunk into my thick head," said Richard. "How was Gillian killed, and why?"

"Rowbottom did that," said Fane. "Medley tells me they found some morphia tablets in his pocket. She was pretty ill when she arrived, and we had Tucker out right away. Tucker prescribed the sedative and wasn't surprised that she slept so long. But Rowbottom had given her the morphia—probably told her it was aspirin—and we'll find that she had it just before they arrived. We left her alone, as Tucker told us to, and when the morphia took effect no one noticed it.

"I don't think there's any mystery about the motive," he went on. "I think we'll find that she knew Pete Dunn was involved, and let something slip out when in the car with Tom. Raymond may have told her something about it before he was killed. She was terrified, of course, and hardly knew what she was doing. She knew there was something in the deed-box and tried to open it. What she didn't know, I think, was that Raymond had had fake jewels made, locked them away, and buried the real diamonds in the garden."

Martin said, "Well, well!"

"The Guildford police found a newly dug patch, investigated, and found them. We know how the chase for them started. Oh, Medley told me one other thing. Percy Mellor's talked freely. Raymond was caught in London by Garrett and others of the gang, and killed at the garage.

"The real puzzle was why you two boys were involved. It happened like this. Tom and Pete were in a jam. They'd killed Raymond, and the body was at Mellor's garage. Mellor wanted them to get rid of it at once. Pete was scared, too, because he'd gathered from Barbara that Robertson was after him, and wanted to get the body down to the cottage—he could dump it in the sea at night. Tom knew all about this, and when Richard first asked him about the car it seemed a heaven-sent chance. Mellor would sell it cheap, the body would be put in the back, Pete would persuade you to come straight here, and borrow the car for an hour, while you two were at home. But first he wanted to get the diamonds from Raymond's house, so he arranged to be picked up at Guildford. At the same time he arranged to meet Barbara there, wanting to find out more about Robertson.

" Then he saw Robertson in Guildford, and that's what upset all his plans. Obviously Robertson was on his track, although Robertson had not even told Barbara. Pete didn't want to draw Robertson's attention to Blond Beauty, so he let you two boys go on alone—as he thought. He had a shock when you went to Raymond's house."

" *I'll* say he did," breathed Richard.

" Pete decided to disappear, and make out he was kidnapped," went on Fane. " Robertson was his danger, and it's my guess that he had already planned to kill him then. Meanwhile he had a bit of luck. You rang up Tom and asked him to bring Gillian down—and Tom volunteered to check up at the cottage. That stopped you from going to look for Pete at the cottage, which was his perfect sanctuary.

" No doubt Pete was waiting for his opportunity to reappear and borrow the Buick to dump the body—but you found that too quickly for him. Now all his plans had gone wrong, and—well, you know the rest."

" How did he fool us with his voice? " asked Richard.

" He'd simply learned to assume another voice—using that of another of the gang whom you met on the road during the attack. It's quite easy, if you go the right way about it."

" Well, well! " breathed Richard.

" Don't say you're speechless," said Martin dryly. " Any idea who the man was on the road who held me up? "

" Us," corrected Richard.

" One of the gang, according to Mellor. He rated higher than most of them, and was just right for a job like that."

223

He stood up, and went across to his wife.

" Tired, darling? '

" I am, sweet."

" Let's go up," said Fane.

Five minutes after they'd gone, Richard found an excuse to leave Martin and Barbara together.

They didn't waste their time.